PACIFIC CROSSING

OTHER BOOKS BY GARY SOTO

Taking Sides
Neighborhood Odes
Baseball in April and Other Stories

PACIFIC

SCHOLASTIC INC.

New York   Toronto   London   Auckland   Sydney

CROSSING

GARY SOTO

Copyright © 1992 by Gary Soto.
All rights reserved. Published by Scholastic Inc., 555 Broadway,
New York, NY 10012, by arrangement with
Harcourt Brace & Company.
Printed in the U.S.A.
ISBN 0-590-48996-8

7 8 9 10   40   3/0

For Hector Torres and Robin Ganz—
critics with heart

PACIFIC CROSSING

1

LINCOLN MENDOZA WAS startled awake by a strong jolt and the sound of his plastic cup of 7Up sliding across the fold-down tray in front of him. For a second he didn't know where he was. He felt groggy. Another jolt, and he remembered he was thirty-seven thousand feet above the earth, on his way to Japan with his lifelong friend, his blood, his *carnal,* his neighbor from the *barrio,* his number-one man on the basketball floor at Franklin Junior High—Tony Contreras. They were both on a jumbo jet for the first time.

"Please be sure your seatbelts are securely fastened," a tinny voice said over the loudspeaker. The instructions were repeated in Japanese—or so Lincoln assumed, because the Japanese passengers began to fumble with their seatbelts.

Lincoln nudged Tony. Tony's eyes were half-open, and a ribbon of drool was starting to flow from the corner of his mouth. He sighed and shifted away from Lincoln and up against the shoulder of the woman next to him.

"Wake up, man. We're almost there," Lincoln said. "You're drooling."

"No," Tony muttered. "The game ain't started yet."

"What game?" Lincoln asked, chuckling.

Tony was dreaming, gripping a crushed napkin. His knee jerked, like Lincoln's dog Flaco's legs jerked when he traveled through his doggish dreams.

Lincoln let Tony sleep. He drained the soda in his cup, the ice cubes now as small as aspirins. He finished Tony's soda as well and turned to look out the window. The Pacific Ocean was silver in the glare of the late-afternoon sun. In the distance, an island lay in a bluish haze.

When the stewardess came down the aisle, Lincoln asked her when they would arrive. She smiled, and said it would be another hour. She took the boys' cups.

Lincoln sighed and threw his head back into his seat. He had read two books, three battered issues of *Sports Illustrated*, and the in-flight magazine, though it was mostly in Japanese. He had played cards and won $1.50 from Tony, all in nickels and dimes. He had started a crossword puzzle but given up because it had to do with biology terms, which reminded him of school. He had eaten three times and watched a movie that was funny but not so funny that he laughed out loud. And in the boredom of the eight-hour flight he had even listened to the classical-music station on his earphones. Lincoln had never known that sitting down could be so tiring.

He looked out the window. The island was now farther away. The sunlight on the silver water was blinding. Lincoln lowered the shade, tilted his head, and went back to sleep.

2

BEFORE THE END of his seventh-grade year, Lincoln and his mother had moved from Sycamore, a suburb that blazed with the boredom of television and weekend barbecues with his mother's yuppie friends. He had left Columbus Junior High and returned to Franklin in San Francisco. He liked that. He had been reunited with Tony, his friend from childhood, the friend who had kicked Lincoln's baby teeth out—or so the story went, a story that was rehashed by the families every Christmas.

Lincoln and his mother settled in Noe Valley near the Mission District, where Lincoln had spent his first twelve years. They were in the city, but away from the rumbles, break-ins, graffitied walls, loud barroom music, *cholos* in wino shoes, *veteranos* with tattooed arms and pinkish scars, and the scuttling litter of Mission and Twenty-fourth. They settled in a two-bedroom apartment off Dolores Street. His mother was happy because there was a small backyard where she could work the earth into neat rows of petunias, daffodils, and tulips. And she almost jumped up and down with excitement when a single tomato plant took root and reached pathetically skyward for its circle of sunshine.

Before they moved back Lincoln had grown moody. He loathed the suburbs. He had even given up doing his homework. Instead, he played his Hammer cassettes with the volume boosted so high that the walls of his house shook and neighbors complained. He had gotten into fights at school, some he'd won and others—particularly the one against Meathead Bukowski—he'd lost.

Lincoln had become the boyfriend of a girl named Monica, but her father didn't like him. Her mother wasn't too happy with him either, especially after his bike ran over a row of her flowers. He tried to make the flowers stand back up, but they were goners.

He felt bad after he and Monica had broken up. He had cut lawns and washed cars to buy her a Raiders' jacket. When he gave it to her, wrapped in Christmas paper even though it wasn't Christmas, she cried and hugged him. He was amazed how hot tears were when one slid from her cheek and landed on his forearm.

But her parents had made her give the jacket back, and now she was gone. The jacket was hanging in Lincoln's closet, limp as a flag with no wind.

After Lincoln and his mom moved back to San Francisco in January, he began to study *shorinji kempō,* a Japanese martial art, at the Soto Zen Center. He had discovered the center one Saturday after he and Tony, *barrio* brothers in red sneakers, got on the wrong bus and ended up in Japantown. They kicked around for a while, looking at the vases, lacquer boxes, and pearls in store windows. They bought a box of popcorn and watched girls. They stood among a small cluster of onlookers watching a second-rate magician yank scarves from his sleeve. They watched the cops haul the magician away—a public nuisance because he was pulling down bucks from the crowd.

While walking up Pine Street, they heard grunting sounds. They looked up and saw a blood red sign: two combatants and the words *Shorinji Kempō.* They followed the grunts and yells down a hallway and were surprised to come to a room full of people working out in white uniforms.

The *sensei,* a large, barrel-chested Japanese man whose face shone with sweat, welcomed them by pointing to a row of folding chairs along the wall. Their hands squeezed into fists, Lincoln and Tony sat and watched, excited by the kicks, punches, and obviously painful pins and throws. The next week they were taking classes.

Tony quit after two months, but Lincoln stayed, advancing to *sankyu*—brown belt—in six months.

Shorinji kempō didn't have lots of colored belts. A student went from white to brown, with no rainbow stops in between. The school didn't go to tournaments, believing that martial art was to be used in a wicked chance meeting in the streets, not as a game for spectators.

Back with his friends at Franklin Junior High, Lincoln improved his grades from C's to A's. He turned down the volume of his stereo and did the dishes whenever his mother asked. He was happy. His dog, Flaco, was happy. His mother was happy and even thinking of marrying her boyfriend, Roy, a guy with bum knees but a good heart.

One day at school while Lincoln was in metal shop welding two pieces of pipe together, the teacher, Mr. Parish, his mouth full of half-chomped sandwich, called, "Mendoza. Mr. Ayala wants to see you."

Mr. Ayala was the principal, an ex-cop who had worked the Haight–Ashbury during San Francisco's hippie days. He was tough, and proud of the ridged knife scar on his forearm. Few boys talked back to him, but when one did, Mr. Ayala would push him against the wall, a huge hand around the boy's skinny neck, and hiss, "Wise guy, huh?"

Lincoln was baffled by the summons. He dipped the pipe into a trough of gray water, sending up a cloud of metallic steam that stung his nose. He took off his apron and washed his hands, wondering what he had done wrong.

As he walked across the lawn to Principal Ayala's office, he searched his mind for a clue to his fall from grace. He was certain his record was clean. Then he stopped in his tracks as he recalled that yesterday at break he and Tony had gotten an armful of empty milk cartons and hurled them one by one at the mouth of a garbage can. They had joked and played; and when the bell sounded, the milk cartons were left on the ground, oozing white dribbles of milk. What was the big deal? Lincoln thought. But, feeling guilty, he gathered pieces of litter—gum wrappers, Popsicle sticks, paper cups, and crushed milk cartons—as he made his way to the office.

But the smiling, pencil-tapping Mr. Ayala sat Lincoln down and told him that he wasn't in trouble.

"What do you think of Japan?" the principal asked. It was still morning, but his face showed the traces of a five o'clock shadow. His tie was loose, and the cuffs of his shirt were rolled up. His scar was pink in the morning light.

"It's far away," Lincoln responded doubtfully. "They make good cars."

"Wise guy, huh?" Mr. Ayala said, smirking. He explained that a school district in Japan was looking for exchange students for the summer. The student would not have to go to school; he would just stay with a family. The principal had thought of Lincoln because he knew he was taking "some kind of karate."

Lincoln was curious. His mind formed an image of a dojo and a *sensei* sitting in meditation before a bowl of incense. He pictured snowcapped mountains and cherry blossoms parachuting from black branches.

He pictured himself as a boy warrior in a white *gi* stained with the blood of enemies.

"You mean I could go to Japan? Me?" Lincoln asked.

"Yes, you. You'll be an exchange student. You know, a goodwill gesture," Mr. Ayala remarked. He bent a paper clip.

Just then Tony walked into the office looking guilty and smelling of hair oil. Tony seemed to be about to confess to doing something wrong when Lincoln whispered, *"Cállate.* You ain't in trouble."

The principal laughed. "You think you're busted, huh, Tony?" Mr. Ayala said as he pointed Tony to a chair. "And what do *you* think of Japan?"

Tony rubbed his chin. "They make good cars, I guess." His eyes were shining. "Am I right?"

"Another wise guy, huh?" Mr. Ayala said, smiling so the lines on his face deepened. He told Tony about the student-exchange program. He said that he was nominating them because they had shown an interest in Japan by taking martial arts.

"Your grades are crummy," Mr. Ayala said as he opened the folder that held Tony's school records. "But it could do you good to see another country. I want you to make us proud. *¿Entiendes?"*

Lincoln and Tony nodded.

"I'll talk with your parents," Mr. Ayala said. He threw the paper clip at the wastebasket. He missed by a foot, easy. "There will be costs involved. Six hundred dollars for airfare."

"Six hundred?" they both said.

"Don't worry. The PTA will pay for half. You two better go cut some lawns."

Lincoln and Tony left the office bewildered. They had seldom been invited anywhere, and now they were being invited to Japan.

"But I quit *kempō*," Tony said.

"He doesn't know that. Don't say anything."

Lincoln punched Tony in the arm and returned to metal shop, wondering how he and Tony were going to get the money for airfare when sometimes it was difficult to get bus fare. That was the only drawback. Too bad it was such a big one. Maybe his mother would give him some of her savings. He would have to treat her nice for the rest of the century, if not longer.

That night Lincoln told his mother about the student-exchange program. "But it's going to cost us at least three hundred for airfare," he added.

Lincoln's mother was happy for her son. When she was his age, fourteen, she had wanted to go to France as an exchange student, but her family hadn't had the money to send her.

"Money grows on trees," she said, eyes twinkling. "You're going, *mi'jo*."

Lincoln knew what that meant. In her bedroom his mother had hung the key to their safe on the limb of a ficus plant. When the time came, she would snatch that key off the limb and open the safe.

At Tony's house, the family's savings were kept in the refrigerator, smashed in the back of the freezer compartment between a package of frozen peas and a

10

one-eyed salmon that Tony's uncle had caught in Alaska.

Both boys would go to Japan with wads of spending money, because both mothers knew how to save and save, even on rainy days.

———~~———

THE JET DIPPED, and its engines rumbled as its speed slowed. Lincoln woke to see Tony looking at him.

"You got *moco* in your eyes," Tony told him, rubbing his own eyes.

Lincoln wiped his eyes and yawned with a hand over his mouth.

"What time is it?" Lincoln asked. "I feel lousy."

"I don't know, bro'. Seems like we were born on this jet. Is Japan near the moon?"

The Fasten Seatbelts sign lit up and the stewardess came down the aisle, speaking in Japanese, then English, collecting empty cups and glasses.

"She forgot us Spanish-speaking *gente*," Tony quipped. "*Señorita, mi amigo es muy feo y un tonto también.*"

The woman smiled, her eyes crinkling into triangles. "*No, chavalo, su amigo es lindo y listo.*"

Lincoln and Tony looked at each other, big-eyed with surprise.

"Fresh! She knows Spanish!" they said. They laughed and looked out the window, where a flower of lights from Tokyo glowed against the night sky. Soon they could distinguish buildings, and large freighters docked in the harbor. The jet slowly descended through wispy clouds. They could make out houses, hills, factories, a bridge, and a river of lights—cars on a freeway. They could see a train and, as they dropped lower, a Japanese sign advertising Coca-Cola.

As the jet landed, the passengers sighed, and some clapped. It had been a long journey—almost nine hours of stale air, cramped seats, and magazines read and reread.

They went through customs, and the white-gloved officers searched handbags and carry-ons. Passports were brought out. Tony joked about being caught and frisked by *la migra*. He kept joking until Lincoln told him to shut up.

"Can't you think of anything else to say?" Lincoln scolded.

"Yeah, what am I doing here? I don't take martial arts. You're the dude. I coulda been workin' at my uncle Rudy's restaurant and makin' money instead of spendin' it."

"Who wants to work? You got your whole life to do that."

"Yeah, you're right," Tony agreed.

They went through customs without a hitch. As they walked up a ramp to meet their host families, Lincoln hoped that he and Tony would see each other soon.

Back in California, they had taken a week of orientation classes with other young people going to Japan through the same exchange program. Now they were on their own. They were the only students staying in Atami, a small farming village three hours outside Tokyo. Lincoln was with the Ono family, and Tony would be with the Inaba family. Both lived on tiny one-acre farms. Lincoln knew that his sponsor worked for the railroad, that his wife took care of their small farm, and that they had a son near his age. He looked forward to his days in Japan. He wanted to study *kempō*, and to learn to speak some Japanese. He had six weeks to do it.

"This is weird," Lincoln heard Tony say as he was swallowed up by a cluster of people. The whole Inaba family—father, mother, and son—smiled, bowed over and over, and welcomed Tony with little gifts wrapped in beautifully designed paper.

3

MR. ONO BOWED and asked, "Mr. Lincoln Mendoza?"

Lincoln stood before a small man with watery eyes. His dignified face was lined and dark. It bespoke the long haul of providing for a family. Lincoln bowed a little more deeply than his sponsor. "Yes, I'm Lincoln Mendoza. Thank you for having me."

"Good," Mr. Ono remarked. He pumped Lincoln's outstretched hand, and Lincoln could feel the power of a working man's grip.

Shouldering his flight bag, Lincoln turned and saw Tony giving a *raza*-style handshake to Mr. Inaba. Tony was laughing, and his sponsor was smiling and asking to see the handshake again.

"¡Órale, Papi!" Tony screamed. "You got it down!"

Nine thousand miles from home, thought Lincoln, and Tony's acting like a regular *vato*. Lincoln called, "See ya in town," and Tony, playing up the homeboy image, raised a clenched fist and shouted, "¡Viva la Raza!"

Lincoln hurried alongside Mr. Ono. They walked briskly, sliding between the rush of travelers racing to catch their flights.

They gathered the luggage, and only in the car did Mr. Ono say in near-perfect English, "My family is waiting at home." Lincoln's head jerked as the car shifted into second, then third, rumbling from a bad muffler.

Lincoln watched Tokyo unfold from the freeway. The evening skyline was bright with neon and skyscrapers. Street-long oil tankers lay docked in the harbor, where the moonlight failed to shimmer on the dark water. A tall radio antenna stood on a hill, a stalk of red lights blinking slowly. Lincoln thought Tokyo resembled San Francisco, where houses stood against the backdrop of the Bay.

The billboards on the side of the freeway advertised in *kanji*, Japanese writing, with now and then an English word like "shampoo" or "luxury." He couldn't understand the *kanji* but could easily understand that they were announcing cars, cigarettes, beer, and liquor—the same products as in the United States.

The drivers were just as crazy as in San Francisco,

but the honking cars seemed quieter, less obnoxious. The traffic was stop-and-go until they reached a four-lane highway that would take them out of the city.

"Tokyo's like America," Lincoln said, smiling and trying to make conversation. "You know, we even have our own Cherry Blossom Festival. In San Francisco."

"Yes," Mr. Ono said, braking so hard that Lincoln had to hold on to the dashboard. "Yes, yes." A car was stalled in the left lane. Mr. Ono wiggled his steering wheel as he maneuvered dangerously into the next lane.

"I'm from San Francisco," Lincoln continued. "We're right on a bay like Tokyo."

"Yes, but America is very large," Mr. Ono said as he swerved back into the left lane, his eyes looking in the mirror. "It is big as the sky." A car honked at them, but Mr. Ono ignored it.

Big as the sky, Lincoln thought. He didn't know how to respond. He turned his attention to the harbor and its huge freighters weighed down with exports. Lincoln thought of his mother's car, a Maxima made in Japan, and how it was closing in on a hundred thousand miles without a breakdown. It was dented on one side, and the back window was cracked from when Tony accidentally slammed it with a bat.

The muggy air made Lincoln feel lousy. Sweat blotched his underarms and pasted his shirt to his skin. It was July, one of the hottest times in Tokyo, and the cement and asphalt still blazed from the punishing daytime sun. Lincoln looked at a Coca-Cola sign and ran his tongue over his lips, thirsting for one precious swallow.

Mr. Ono noticed; he reached into the backseat and pulled a bottle from a bag. "*Ramune*. It's good. Can you say?"

Lincoln took the bottle and turned it over. "*Ramune*," he said under his breath.

Mr. Ono opened the bottle by pushing down on the top, dislodging a marble stopper. Lincoln took a long, serious swallow, which cleared his throat and made him feel good. He looked at the characters on the label but couldn't figure out if the drink was soda or juice.

"What is it again?"

"*Ramune*. It's good for you, Lincoln-kun."

Lincoln shrugged his shoulders, drank until the bottle was empty, and placed the bottle in the backseat. "That was good." He beamed. "Thanks."

Soon the city gave way to a patchwork of small farms rippling with stalks of rice lit by the July moonlight. As the car picked up speed, the fender rattled. Lincoln had noticed when they got in the car that the fender was old and buckled. He had seen that Mr. Ono was dressed plainly and that his hands were as rough as the hands of Lincoln's uncle Ray, a radiator man. He had imagined that everyone in Japan was doing well, living off the riches of high-tech computers and first-rate cars. But he had been wrong.

In the dark, Lincoln could just make out the features of Mr. Ono puffing on a cigarette, the red glow

17

of the ash brightening his face. He looked like a worker, stubble on his chin, eyes sagging from fatigue. He looked Mexican, dark and tough skinned from years of work. Lincoln pulled down the car's visor and looked at himself in the mirror. His skin was unblemished, his eyes bright, and his hair black and shiny as a polished shoe.

The hum of the car's engine lulled Lincoln into a drowsy stupor. He was tired from the long flight, as well as from the night before, when he hadn't been able to sleep from anticipation of the trip. He had turned over and over restlessly, his mind loaded with an image of Japan: a dojo swept clean and a faint aura of incense in the air. Now he was in Japan, and Japan looked more like San Francisco than like the calendars his mom got from Sumitomo Bank. To Lincoln, Tokyo was disappointingly modern.

Lincoln had started wondering about Japan after he had begun taking *kempō*, and he had become interested in the history and culture after he and his mother had gone to a festival of Japanese movies. His favorite movie was *Yojimbo*, about a blind swordsman who slashed evil from a small village. But Tokyo was nothing like the movie. Not one woman was wearing a kimono; not one man was walking in *geta*, wooden sandals.

Lincoln fell asleep. When he woke, the car was pulling into a driveway. A cat's eyes were lit by the headlights. The sky was no longer filled with the harsh, blistering light of the city. It was black, stars pulsating above. Crickets chattered in the grasses. A dog barked

18

in the distance. A radio was playing classical music. They had driven nearly 150 miles, and Tokyo was gone.

Lincoln ran a moist hand over his face, stretched, and yawned. He felt dirty, his shirt was stiff with dried sweat, and his mouth was sour from not having brushed his teeth since breakfast, many time zones ago, when he'd been in California. He opened the car door and lowered a leg stiffly to the ground. He was "home," and home was a small western-style house on a tiny farm. He could smell the vegetables in the field. He could smell the faint stinks of chickens and compost. The moon hung, silver and round as a nickel, between two trees.

Lincoln got out of the car slowly, trying his best to show his happiness to the Onos and their son, Mitsuo.

"Welcome, Lincoln," Mrs. Ono said, bowing. "You must be tired."

Lincoln bowed and said, "Yes, I'm tired. Thank you for having me."

Mrs. Ono seemed taller than her husband. She reminded Lincoln of his own mother, big-boned and dark, with a smile that made him smile back. She was dressed in jeans and a plaid blouse, and her hair was pinned back into a bun.

Lincoln couldn't help himself; he blurted out, "You look like my mom."

"My English is not so good," the mother said as she helped with the luggage. "Please say again."

"Oh, I mean, thank you for having me," Lincoln

said, and he bit his tongue. He shouldered his backpack and took the luggage from Mrs. Ono. "I can do it." Lincoln waddled under the heaviness of the luggage as he followed the Onos into the house.

Only when the family stared at Lincoln's shoes did he realize that he should take them off. He banged his head with the heel of his palm and said, "Oops, sorry." They smiled, and Mrs. Ono handed him a pair of slippers.

"Would you like something to drink?" Mitsuo asked. Mitsuo was as tall as Lincoln. But while Lincoln's hair was long, almost straggly, Mitsuo's hair was cropped to almost nothing. He was strong. When he took the luggage from Lincoln, his biceps tightened into globes of veined muscle. His T-shirt was stretched over his chest, showing two plates of muscle and flesh.

"*Ramune*, please," Lincoln said.

The mother and son looked at each other, surprised. Mitsuo went to the kitchen for four *ramune* and they settled in the living room. They looked at each other, smiling and drinking. Lincoln's arms felt limp, his head heavy as a boulder, and his eyes small from lack of sleep.

In careful English Mitsuo asked, "Do you play baseball?"

"No, basketball. But I like baseball. I played Little League for two years."

"Basketball is not so popular here. Baseball is our game. I play the outfield."

While Lincoln nursed his drink, the heaviness of sleep settled on him. He rubbed his eyes, yawned, and sat up straight, trying to keep awake. His host family seemed ready for Lincoln to tell them something about himself. "Baseball. I, ah . . ." Lincoln couldn't concentrate; his mind kept sliding into fatigue. "Sports, ah—I like movies . . ."

"Do you like the San Francisco Giants? We have the Tokyo Giants."

"Yes, plenty of times," Lincoln responded, thinking he had been asked if he had seen the Giants play at Candlestick Park. He drained his drink and watched his host family talk, their mouths moving as they asked questions. Lincoln opened his mouth into a yawn as wide as a hat. He fell asleep on the couch, an empty bottle of *ramune* in his hands.

4

LINCOLN WOKE TO the buzz of a fly circling above him. He slowly opened his eyes, stared at the ceiling, and muttered to himself, "I'm in Japan."

He rolled out of his *futon* and tried to get up but sat back down, feeling dizzy and lethargic. He lay back with a sigh, and after a few minutes of staring at the hypnotic figure eights of the circling fly, he fell asleep again. When he woke a second time, Mitsuo was standing over him, pounding his fist into a baseball glove. The room was hot, sunlight slanting in from an open window. Two flies were circling the air where there had been only one.

"Lincoln-kun, are you awake?"

Lincoln propped himself up on his elbows, blinking sleep from his eyes. "Yeah. I was tired from the flight. What time is it?"

"Lunchtime. Do you like *rāmen*? *Haha* is in the field. *Chichi* is working at the station."

"Who?"

" '*Haha*' is 'Mother,' and '*Chichi*' is 'Father,' " Mitsuo explained. He placed his glove in the closet and pulled back the curtain so that sunlight flooded the room. "Come on, let's eat."

Lincoln rose, washed quickly in the bathroom, and joined Mitsuo in the kitchen. They ate in silence, watching each other and smiling now and then. Lincoln liked Mitsuo. "You are good with *hashi*," Mitsuo complimented.

"You mean chopsticks?"

"Yes, 'chopsticks.' Very funny word. We have spoons if you need one."

Lincoln sucked in a cheekful of noodles. He wanted to tell Mitsuo that he ate mostly using a tortilla, but how, on the first day, could he explain that he was both Mexican and American? He drained the broth of his *rāmen*. Maybe later I'll tell them about Mexican food, he thought as he wiped his mouth with a paper napkin.

Mitsuo got up and said, "I have to get back to work. You rest."

"No, I'll help," Lincoln said, taking his bowl to the sink.

"You are our guest."

"No, please. I want to help."

Mituso thought for a moment. "OK, but let me

23

get you something." He left and returned with a long-sleeved work shirt.

"Here." Mitsuo handed Lincoln the shirt. "The flies will bite if you don't wear a shirt. And use this hat."

Lincoln put on the hat and looked at himself reflected in the kitchen window. He liked what he saw. "My mom would be proud. She used to work in the fields."

"Your mother is a farmer?" Mitsuo asked, lacing up his boots. "Here, wear Father's boots."

"No, but she used to pick grapes when she was little. Now she works in an office." Lincoln picked up the boots, whose tips were curled, and stuffed his feet into them.

The two of them joined Mrs. Ono, who was knee-deep in eggplant leaves. The family would harvest in a month, but now, in early July, the eggplant fruits poked through the green growth, still swelling like balloons. The vegetables needed to be weeded, irrigated, and examined for worms.

"*Nasu*," Mitsuo said and pointed to the eggplant.

"*Nasu*," Lincoln repeated.

Lincoln knew nothing about work, though he used to wash his uncle's BMW for money and cut a few lawns. Most of his relatives had once worked in the fields chopping cotton, cutting grapes, and picking oranges, cantaloupes, and almonds on the west side of the San Joaquin Valley. But field work—even in a one-acre patch of eggplant, his least favorite vegetable, and three rows of tomato plants—was something new to Lincoln. He felt proud as he staggered about in oversized boots, a hat shading his eyes from the sun.

Mrs. Ono looked up. "Good morning, Lincoln-kun." She looked skyward. "No, good afternoon."

"I was so sleepy," Lincoln said. And even now, though it was midday, he felt groggy from the flight. "I'm sorry I woke up late."

"It was a long trip," Mrs. Ono said. Her face was hidden in the shadow of her hat; mud clung to her boots. "Did you eat?"

"*Rāmen.*"

"Do you like *rāmen?*"

"Of course," Lincoln said good-naturedly as he took the hoe from her. He saw a ribbon of sweat roll down her cheek, and flakes of dirt on her brow. "You rest. Mitsuo and I will finish up."

"Lincoln-kun would like to help," Mitsuo said.

Mrs. Ono turned to Lincoln. "But you are our guest."

"I want to help, though."

"But if you are a guest, you cannot work. This would be embarrassing for us."

"I'm part of the family," Lincoln countered. "You rest and Mitsuo and I will take over."

Mrs. Ono's face softened with tenderness. She laughed and wiped the sweat from her face. "I have work inside. And dinner to prepare." She left the field, undoing her hat and wiping her neck with a bandanna.

Mitsuo took up a hoe and said, "Like this." He walked between the narrow rows, parting the leaves and gently whacking at the weeds. Lincoln followed, and they hoed in silence, the hot sun riding on their backs.

———〰———

LINCOLN'S LOWER BACK sparked with pain as he leaned his hoe against the shed. The sun hovered in the west, slipping behind the tiled roofs of the neighbors' houses. He had worked for only three hours, but he was exhausted. A cat on the fence watched Lincoln as he sat down and started to unlace his muddy boots. When the cat meowed, Lincoln hissed at him.

"You have to work every day?" Lincoln asked.

"Every day," Mitsuo answered as he unlaced his own mud-caked boots and took off his shirt. "We must."

His first full day in Japan, and the only things he had seen were the purple snouts of eggplant. Lincoln laughed to himself as he drank a bottle of icy *ramune*, his Adam's apple rising and falling with each swallow. He and Mitsuo sat on the *engawa*, the wooden porch that faced the backyard, and eyed the field, each quiet in his own thoughts. The air was heavy, moist, and scented with earth. Over the nearby roofs, Lincoln spied the tallest buildings of Atami. Far away, a car with a bad muffler roared. A neighbor was yelling at a barking dog, and two kids were playing with plastic swords in the street. Lincoln, finishing his drink, was too exhausted to be curious about where he was. He lay back and fell asleep for a few minutes, the bottle in his hand, and woke only when he heard Mitsuo's voice.

26

"Are you tired?"

"A little bit." Lincoln stretched like a cat.

As he lay there, his hands behind his head, Lincoln thought about home. He wasn't homesick yet, but he knew it would come, an overwhelming shadow of sadness that would touch him when he least expected it. Once he had visited his aunt in the Imperial Valley of California, and after three days he was weeping into his pillow, longing for home. He was only eight then. Now he was fourteen and a lot wiser. Still, he knew that he'd get homesick. For now, he was just hot and sticky. And hungry.

"You know, it's probably lunchtime in San Francisco." Lincoln's stomach grumbled, and he wished he could throw his jaw around a cheeseburger.

"What's San Francisco like?"

"It's like Tokyo. But not hot. I thought I was going to die on the way from the airport."

"We hear California has many crazy persons. Is it true?"

"Some. There are some crazy dudes who walk the street."

"Do you have a gun?" Mitsuo asked, rolling the empty bottle of *ramune* over his chest. Its coolness raised a herd of chills on his skin.

Lincoln rose on his elbows and looked at Mitsuo, bewildered. "A gun? I don't even have a car."

"We hear all Americans carry guns."

Lincoln laughed, then stopped. He remembered a *vato loco* from his old street getting shot, all because he hadn't paid a two-dollar bet on a football game. He didn't die, but his knee was shattered. "Yeah, some dudes trip out with guns. But most people are cool."

"Cool? What is 'cool'?"

"It means OK—you know, nice."

"Cool," Mitsuo said, reflecting on the word.

"Where did you learn English?" Lincoln asked.

"School. It's required. America is number one, and Japan is number two, so we must learn your language."

"No, it's the other way around," Lincoln countered as he peeled off his shirt. "You people have got it together. I like your cars."

"Cars are nothing," Mitsuo argued. "Hammer is number one!"

Lincoln laughed. He spread his legs into a V and began to stretch, fingers to toes. Mitsuo had told him that *kempō* practice would begin that evening, and Lincoln wanted to be limber.

The boys were silent for a long time. Two huge crows bickered on a telephone wire, and from the house came the sound of a knife chopping on a wooden block. Then Mitsuo sat up, rolling the bottle across the porch. "Let's go."

"Where?" asked Lincoln, rising slowly and putting on his T-shirt.

"You'll see."

Mitsuo handed Lincoln a pair of *geta*, wooden slippers. "Wear these."

Lincoln turned them over, then slipped them on. He took a few careful steps. Wearing them was like walking on stilts. "They're fresh."

" 'Fresh'?" asked Mitsuo, putting on a clean shirt that had been hanging on the rail of the porch. "You like them, you mean?"

"They're real cool."

"Fresh," Mitsuo muttered as they left the porch, the *karakoro* sound of the *geta* ringing on the stone walk that led to the gate. They waved to Mrs. Ono, who was at the kitchen window. She shouted that they should come home in time for dinner.

5

~~~

LINCOLN AND MITSUO walked briskly between the one-acre fields; almost all of them were thick with the green growth of vegetables. The fields soon gave way to homes and small businesses—bars, restaurants, a cyclery, a fish market, appliance stores. The dirt road gave way to cement sidewalks. The street was crowded with men returning home, ties loosened and white shirts limp from long hours of work.

Atami was a growing farm town. For centuries, its farms had pushed up to the mountains. Apples and pears grew on the foothills. Today Atami's main street was choked with cars and gleaming with tall glass buildings. Bicycles came rattling down the narrow streets and pushed pedestrians against the walls.

Lincoln followed Mitsuo into a building where

the air was moist and thick with the sound of rain. A husky man sat at a counter. His glasses were fogged up, and a newspaper was spread in front of him. He looked up, wiped his glasses, and muttered in Japanese to Mitsuo, who produced some yen.

"What is this place?" Lincoln asked.

"A *sentō*. It's a public bathhouse."

"We're going to take a bath?"

Lincoln trailed after Mitsuo, who was already pulling off his shirt. They entered a small steamy room where men were soaping themselves and rinsing from buckets.

"Here goes," Lincoln said and pulled off his shirt. He was a bit embarrassed when he saw three men sitting in what looked like a shallow swimming pool.

The boys put their clothes in a wicker basket. The *geta* went along the wall.

"I show you," Mitsuo said. "Sit down."

Lincoln sat down on a small wood-slat stool. Mitsuo started to soap and scrub his back in large, swirling circles.

"This is weird. I feel like I'm in a car wash," Lincoln muttered. He had heard about public baths, but he still found it shocking to be in one.

After Mitsuo rinsed him off, Lincoln soaped and scrubbed Mitsuo, who laughed and groaned, "Scrub harder, harder."

They climbed into the tiled tub, Mitsuo nearly jumping in and Lincoln stepping in one leg at a time.

"Man, it's hot as lava," Lincoln hissed. "I'm gonna burn *mis nalgas*."

31

"What's 'nalgas'?" Mitsuo asked as he lowered his body into the water.

"It's your butt."

"*My* butt?"

Lincoln laughed. "No, it's everyone's butt."

Mitsuo gave Lincoln a strange look.

Lincoln was going to try to explain but stopped when he saw Mitsuo waving. Through the puffs of steam, Lincoln caught sight of a naked Mr. Ono, who was saying hello to a friend. Mr. Ono called to Mitsuo, and Mitsuo climbed out of the bath to scrub his father's back. Then both of them joined Lincoln in the tub. He was now red as a crab, his forehead beaded with sweat.

"Lincoln-kun," the father said, "how are you? You look hot."

"I am."

"Good," Mr. Ono said as he threw a handful of water on his face. "The tub is cold. They should turn up the heat."

Mitsuo giggled and said, "Lincoln said it burns his *nalgas.*"

"What is 'nalgas'?" the father asked. His glistening head floated on the surface of the water.

"It's your butt."

"*My* butt? What do you mean, Mitsuo? Teach me."

Lincoln laughed. Mr. Ono was a comedian, like Lincoln's uncle Slic Ric, who was a member of the Chicano comedy act Culture Clash. It was all jokes from that *vato*, and from Mr. Ono it was poker-faced humor, even after a hard day at the railroad. Lincoln had always thought of Japanese people as reserved and serious. Now he was having second thoughts.

Mitsuo and Lincoln started to climb out of the bath. Their bodies were pink from the hot water.

"It's hard to explain," Mitsuo said.

His father waved them off and turned to talk with a man at the other end of the tub.

Lincoln and Mitsuo dressed and left the *sentō* refreshed. They bought Coca-Colas and looked at magazines at a newsstand. Lincoln didn't understand the *kanji*, but was satisfied to look at a comic book of samurai warriors on horseback. Lincoln thumbed through the pages. At the end, some of the warriors were killed, their heads stuck on lances and paraded around a defeated city. Lincoln swallowed and thought, That must hurt.

"Do you know *pachinko?*" Mitsuo asked as he returned his magazine to the rack.

"No," Lincoln answered.

"I'll show you." Mitsuo pulled on Lincoln's arm. They hurriedly crossed the street, which was jammed by a car accident. Two men were standing by their cars, each shouting and seeming to blame the other.

They walked three short blocks and stood looking through a storefront window at what Lincoln thought at first were video games. These were machines for *pachinko,* a kind of upright pinball game. The place reminded Lincoln of his uncle Trino's bar, La Noche de Guadalajara. His uncle used to shove a handful of quarters into Lincoln's shirt pocket and let him play the games, even though he was underage and every-one around him was drinking beer.

Lincoln suggested that they go in and play a game.

"We can't. It's for adults. You have to be at least sixteen," Mitsuo said.

Lincoln took a closer peek. Rows of players, mostly men, hunkered over the machines. The chrome balls fell noisily from one level to the next.

"Aw, man," Lincoln whined. "I wish I could play just one game."

Mitsuo thought a moment, then said, "Let's try."

"Really? You don't think we'll get in trouble?" When Mitsuo shook his head, Lincoln said, "OK, but you lead the way."

They started up the steps, their heads down, trying to look tough. Smoke laced the air. Loud music blared from speakers in the ceiling. They found an open machine and started playing, but within a few minutes they were collared and thrown out.

"Don't try again," the man warned. He was small but thick as a refrigerator. He looked dangerous.

The boys shrugged. Lincoln rubbed his scraped elbow.

"The man is not cool," Mitsuo muttered. Through his cupped hands, he yelled back through the door-way, "You are not cool!"

"Give it to him, the fat slob," Lincoln growled. "I was just starting to like the game."

The man started toward them, but Lincoln and Mitsuo were too fast.

After the *pachinko* parlor, they kicked around the

town, looking in shop windows and following two girls who were eyeing them and giggling. But Lincoln and Mitsuo left the girls alone. They bought bags of pumpkin seeds and walked around eating the seeds, shells and all.

"Our town is small," Mitsuo said. "You will see your friends soon. We have only twenty thousand people in this town."

Lincoln thought of Tony. He was probably either complaining about the field work or teaching his host family to play poker. Tony had learned poker from his older brother, who was a *Mechista* in college, a guy ready to better the world for Chicanos.

Mitsuo pointed to a wooden building with slat windows. "I took judo there but quit." A wind chime banged in the breeze.

"You took judo?" Lincoln asked, excited. "That's bad."

"No, judo is good."

"No, I mean bad. In California, if you like something a lot, then it's bad."

Mitsuo gave Lincoln another strange look. He said, "In Japan, everyone takes judo or *kempō*. I didn't like judo. For me, it was not 'bad.' Baseball is 'bad.'" Mitsuo then pointed to a round man walking down the street. "He's Takahashi-*sensei*. He's OK, but his assistant is mean. He was mean to me because I lost a match at a tournament."

"You went to tournaments? Sounds fun."

"I went to a few, but I wasn't very good."

"Sure you were."

"No, really."

Lincoln let the subject drop because he knew how sensitive he was when a defeat came up in conversation. He recalled the basketball games back home. Except for basketball at school, he had to work hard at everything, even spelling.

They watched the *sensei* open the dojo with a key as large as a can opener. He entered, his shoes in his hand. The door closed behind him, and a light went on.

"I'll show you the *kempō* dojo," Mitsuo said.

"All right!" Lincoln cried.

They hurried through an alley and down three blocks, their mouths full of pumpkin seeds. When Mitsuo stopped, Lincoln nearly bumped into him.

"There," Mitsuo said, pointing.

"Where?" Lincoln asked, confused. He was facing a cement driveway with a border of wild grass.

"There."

"Where?"

"There, Lincoln-kun!"

"You mean this *driveway?*"

"Yes, they practice there and on the lawn. I think they practice at the university in winter."

Lincoln's image of a cleanly swept dojo evaporated like rain on a hot sidewalk. He was disappointed. He had come to Japan expecting to practice on tatami mats in a templelike dojo.

"They practice on concrete," he whispered.

6

WHEN MITSUO AND Lincoln returned home, Mitsuo's father and mother were sitting with a woman on the *engawa*. The woman sat erect, her face composed. All three were drinking iced tea, Mrs. Ono cooling herself with a fan that showed a picture of a baseball team.

Mitsuo gave the woman a short bow and greeted her in Japanese. Lincoln bowed, too.

"Lincoln-kun, this is Mrs. Oyama," the father said. He raised his glass, sipped, and put it down by his feet. "You and Mitsuo worked hard. The field looks tidy."

After a moment of silence, Mrs. Oyama asked, "So, Lincoln, you practice *shorinji kempō?*" Her face was turned away, as if she were asking Mr. Ono.

"Yes," Lincoln answered, his back straight.

"You must be very good. You're so young and strong," Mrs. Oyama said, a smile starting at the corner of her mouth. She was still looking in the direction of Mr. Ono.

"Well, I guess so," Lincoln said, flattered, tightening his fist so that a rope of muscle showed in his forearm. He tried to hold back a smile. "I'm *sankyu* rank."

"*Sankyu.* Very good for your age," Mrs. Oyama said, an eyebrow lifted. She turned to Mrs. Ono and said, "Such a strong boy."

"Oh yes, he worked so hard in the garden today," Mrs. Ono said, fanning the cool air in Lincoln's direction.

He sat straight up, his chest puffed out a little. "Well, I am pretty good. That's what Nakano-*sensei* says. I'll be a black belt when I'm fifteen."

"I'm impressed." Mrs. Oyama beamed, pressing her hands together. "I'm so happy to hear that in America we have dedicated youth."

The telephone rang in the living room. Mitsuo jumped to his feet. Lincoln started to follow, but the adults told him to stay.

"Mitsuo will answer it," Mr. Ono told Lincoln. He lit a cigarette, a wafer of smoke hanging in the air, and asked, "Lincoln-kun, what does your mother do?"

"She's sort of an artist. She has her own company." Lincoln bit his lower lip as he tried to think of what she actually did for a living. "She's a commercial artist. She does work for computer firms."

Mr. Ono shook his head, sighing, "Ah yes."

"And your father?" Mrs. Ono asked.

Lincoln had known this was coming. He had known ever since he'd boarded the jet to come to Japan that he would be asked this question. "He's a police officer," Lincoln said, not adding that he hadn't seen his father in six years. His parents had been divorced since Lincoln was seven, a hurt that had never healed.

The adults looked at each other, nodding their heads. They sipped tea and stirred the air with newspaper shaped into fans.

Mrs. Oyama rose. "I will see you tomorrow, if not sooner," she said to Lincoln and Mitsuo, who had returned from the living room. She bowed to Mr. and Mrs. Ono, thanked them for the tea, and walked down the path to the street.

While they ate fish for dinner, the Ono family helped Lincoln practice some Japanese phrases. He wanted to learn so that when he returned home he could talk in Japanese to his *kempō* instructor. So Mrs. Ono taught him some phrases. "How are you doing? Nice day. Let's eat." Her eyes shone when Lincoln said, *"Ima Atami ni sun'de imasu.* I am now living in Atami."

"You are a strong, smart boy," she said.

On the *engawa* after dinner, Mr. Ono said to Mitsuo, "Take Lincoln to the dojo." Mr. Ono was enjoying a small cup of sake with an evening cigarette. "You are not too tired, are you, Lincoln-kun? It is almost eight o'clock."

"No, not at all," Lincoln said as he left the room

to get his *gi*. He felt good. He was ready to practice, even in a driveway.

Mr. Ono spoke to Mitsuo in Japanese, and Mitsuo turned away, almost laughing.

"What is *Chichi* joking about?" Lincoln asked, smiling as well.

"He is glad you are here," Mitsuo said as he slipped on his *geta*. "I'll take you to *kempō*."

They walked four blocks in silence, and when they arrived at the driveway, Mitsuo turned away, a smile starting on his face. "I will see you in one hour. Have fun."

Puzzled at Mitsuo's smile, Lincoln watched him hurry away, *geta* ringing on the stone walk. Lincoln shrugged his shoulders as he entered the driveway with a fistful of yen, his monthly dues. On his way down the driveway, Lincoln stopped to *gasshō*—salute—to three black belts who were stretching on the lawn, sweat already soaking into the backs of their *gis*. They rose to their feet, saluted to Lincoln, and pointed to the side of the building. Lincoln went around and saw two others changing, a father and son. He changed there as well, folding his clothes neatly and placing his *geta* along the wall. He took off his watch, which glowed in the dark: 8:10.

Everyone was speaking in Japanese. No one paid Lincoln any attention as he joined the others on the lawn. He looked skyward at a plane cutting across the sky, and at that moment he wished he were on that plane.

A light lit the yard, reflecting off a small kidney-shaped pond, set among reeds and bamboo. Lincoln went and looked at the pond. He saw the reflection of his face in the murky water, rippling from long-legged water bugs.

He rejoined the others on the lawn and began stretching and practicing punches and kicks. His chest rose and fell, and his breathing became shallow. In the warm summer air, sweat was already starting to run from his body.

The *sensei* came out of the house, hands raised in a *gasshō*. She smiled and welcomed everyone as they formed two lines.

Lincoln's mouth fell open. It was Mrs. Oyama, whom he had met just before dinner—Oyama-*sensei!* He found a place at the back of the line, his face twisted with worry. Only an hour ago he had been bragging that he was *sankyu* rank, that he was as strong as any kid in the world.

After a formal salute to the spirit of *kempō*, some meditation, and warm-ups, the group finally started basic exercises. Only after basics did Oyama-*sensei* point to Lincoln, and everyone looked in his direction.

Lincoln forced a toothy smile. He hated life at that moment. He wished that he were on that plane, going back home to San Francisco. He promised himself this would be the last time he bragged.

"Lincoln, please," Oyama-*sensei* called, her outstretched hand gesturing for him to come up to the front. "Please tell us about yourself."

I'm a loudmouthed braggart, Lincoln thought; that's what I could tell you about myself.

Sweat streamed down his face, more from embarrassment than from the workout. He walked to the front, where he gave a *gasshō* and told his fellow practitioners—all eight of them—that he was from San Francisco and that he was staying with the Ono family for the summer. When they smiled at him, he felt a little better.

They practiced *juhō*—grabs and pinning techniques—and *embu*—planned attacks. He tried his best. He didn't want these adult black belts to think he was sorry, just because he was from America and a fourteen-year-old brown belt. His punches and kicks snapped against his *gi*. His arm locks were executed quickly, but not with the ease of the adults'.

Lincoln had never worked out on grass before. In San Francisco, he had practiced on linoleum. He liked the way the grass tickled the bottoms of his feet. He also liked having the grass to cushion his falls; he fell a lot when he practiced with the advanced belts. He was thrown and twisted into painful holds, his face pressed harshly against the grass. He got up quickly when they let go, and he didn't let on that his arm felt like a drumstick being torn from the body of a chicken.

When class ended at 9:30, Oyama-*sensei* called him aside. "Lincoln-kun, you are a good boy. Strong."

"I'm not that strong," he said, this time not wanting to brag about himself. He was still warm from the workout, and his chest was rising and falling. Grass clung to his *gi* and his tousled hair.

"You are very good. In six weeks, if you practice hard, we will see about a promotion." One side of her face was hidden in the dark; the other side glowed in the porch light. Her eyes gave away nothing.

Lincoln started to walk away, but she called him back. "Lincoln-kun, you must shave your hair."

"My hair?" he asked, touching the hair around his ears.

"Yes, it must be gone."

———〜———

LINCOLN CHANGED FROM his *gi* to his street clothes and was greeted by Mitsuo, who was waiting in the driveway.

"How come you didn't tell me?" Lincoln asked. "She's the *sensei*, and you didn't tell me. That was cold."

"Sorry, Lincoln, but Father wanted to make a joke. He likes you." Mitsuo thought for a moment, then asked, "What is 'cold'?"

" 'Cold' is, is—I don't know how to explain it. But that was a 'cold' shot," Lincoln said as the two of them walked down the street, their *geta* ringing in unison. "Yeah, your dad is a wise guy."

"Yes, he is sometimes very wise," Mitsuo agreed.

Lincoln stopped in his tracks and was about to explain "wise guy" and the Three Stooges, but he was too tired. It had been a long day in Japan.

The stores were closed. A few cars passed in the street, silent as cats. Only a small neon light glowed in a bar window. They tiptoed over and looked inside, where men sat playing *go*, an ancient board game similar to checkers, or talking in dark corners.

"Just like California," Lincoln said.

"Really?"

"Yeah. People get off work and get ripped—some people, at least."

"My father used to come here, but he doesn't anymore. He likes it better at home."

Lincoln wanted to tell Mitsuo about his father—about his lack of a father—but didn't know how. In the United States, it was not uncommon to come from a broken home. But in Japan families all seemed to be intact—father, mother, children, all walking down the street together. In the *sentō*, fathers scrubbed their children, and, in turn, the children scrubbed their fathers with all their might. It wasn't Lincoln's fault that his parents' marriage hadn't worked out. Still, at times he felt lonely and embarrassed.

They walked home. Lincoln showered and then went out to the *engawa* to join Mitsuo, who was relacing his baseball mitt after having taken out some of the padding.

"This is my favorite mitt," Mitsuo said proudly. "My grandfather gave it to me."

"Nice." The night was quiet. A cat strode the thin rail of a bamboo fence, his tail waving in the moonlight. The neighbors were watching television. The vegetable garden rustled in the breeze. Lincoln felt tired but happy. He was already feeling at home.

7

THE NEXT DAY, Lincoln and Mitsuo worked in the field again, this time hauling buckets of water to irrigate the rows. They worked hard, shirtless. Flies nibbled at their backs, and Lincoln and Mitsuo complained and cursed their luck. But secretly they felt good.

At lunch, they sat on the *engawa* eating *nigirimeshi*—rice balls—and drinking a pitcher of iced tea.

"They're good," Lincoln said as he chomped into the rice balls.

"But wouldn't you rather have a hamburger?" Mitsuo asked.

Lincoln shook his head. "You know what I'd like to have? A burrito."

"A burrito?"

Lincoln cleared his throat. "A tortilla with *frijoles*."

Mitsuo tilted his head curiously and asked, "What is 'tortilla'? And that other word—'freeholies'?"

Lincoln licked his lips and drank long and hard from his glass. A stream of tea ran down his chest and pooled in his belly button. He laughed as he wiped his belly. "It's this way, Mitsuo. I'm from California, but I'm Mexican-American, and that's Mexican-American food."

"Mexican and American," Mitsuo said slowly, reflecting on the words. "Are you from two countries?"

"Sort of. Just like you. If you came to the United States, you would be Japanese-American."

"Ah, I understand. Then you are from Mexico."

"No. From California."

"Then your mother is from Mexico?"

"No. She's from California, too."

"Then it must be your father?"

"No, not him either. It's my grandparents."

Mitsuo looked at Lincoln and said, "Family history is very complicated. My father says we're from a samurai line."

"Really?" Lincoln asked, his interest piqued.

"He says so, but I doubt it. Our family has been farmers for centuries. I don't think we have samurai blood. My father is always making things up."

"I can relate. My mom says that we're descendants of Aztec warriors. But look at my legs—skinny!" He gripped his thighs with both hands.

After lunch, the two boys left with fishing poles and tackle. Just outside town, they hopped a ride on the back of a produce truck, and three dusty miles later they jumped off when the truck slowed at a railroad crossing. Only now aware that they had ridden his truck, the driver cursed and shook a fist at them.

Lincoln and Mitsuo ran away, their poles jumping about on their shoulders. They walked another mile, the sun beating down on their heads, and entered waist-high brush where a shallow river flowed over small rocks. They threw themselves on the bank, moons of sweat under each arm.

"Man, it's hot," Lincoln grumbled. "Is it always like this?"

"In the summer," Mitsuo said, opening the tackle box.

They dipped their faces in the water but didn't drink. They flicked off their *geta* and let their food cool in the water. They felt calm. A wind had picked up, rustling some low-lying brush where two sparrows bickered.

"Is the Mississippi River very big?" Mitsuo asked, splicing a worm on his hook.

"Very big. But I've never seen it." Lincoln recalled classroom spelling bees when the word had stumped the boys' team. The girls had laughed at the boys who either put in one too many *p*'s or not enough *s*'s. Lincoln figured that the word "Mississippi" should be banned from the English language.

"One day I'd like to go to America."

"Yeah. You and I could hang out together. You could stay with us."

Mitsuo smiled. " 'Hang out,' " he murmured. "Nice words." He stared at a ripple on the water.

"You'd like it. We can get my mom to take us to Great America. The roller coaster is tough."

Lincoln stared at the water. His mind drifted to Oyama-*sensei*. She must have a sense of humor, he thought. Or why would she visit the Onos and not let on that she's a *kempō* master? Lincoln smiled to himself. When his line went taut, he was ready and rose to his feet. He reeled the line in and found the hook snagged with nothing but slimy grass.

They fished until two old men arrived and told them to go away, that it was *their* fishing spot. The men sat down with tired sighs and brought out a lunch and bottles of beer, which they rolled into the river to cool. Lincoln wanted to argue with them, but Mitsuo touched his arm and begged, "Let's not. We didn't catch anything anyhow."

One of the old men cast, and almost immediately a fish came up, its back shimmering in the sunlight. The old man grinned at Lincoln, showing his black teeth as if to say, We're the fishermen.

From the river the boys returned to the main highway, where they got a ride in the back of a truck loaded with chickens on the way to restaurants in Atami.

"It's sad," Lincoln said. "They're gonna have their throats cut."

The chickens blinked their small eyes at Lincoln and Mitsuo, and fluttered their wings occasionally. Only when the truck dipped into a pothole did the chickens cluck. Only when the truck braked did they panic and beat their wings against the wooden sides of the crates.

When the truck pulled into town, the boys jumped off and waved to the driver, who waved back. Lincoln couldn't help himself—he waved to the chickens. One of them seemed to raise a wing in salute—*adios, amigo.*

They had started up the street and were skipping over puddles where the merchants had washed the storefronts when Lincoln heard, "Hey, Linc, it's your *carnal.*" Lincoln stopped in his tracks and slowly turned around. It was Tony, in a blue-and-white *yukata,* a long robe, and *geta* on his feet. His hair was shaved so he looked like a monk.

"Tony!" Lincoln screamed. They ran to each other and shook hands *raza*-style. Lincoln raked his hand over Tony's hair and fingered the robe. "Yeah, check this out. You look like a skinny Yojimbo. How'd you get the haircut? I gotta get mine cut for *kempō.*"

"*¡Pues sí! Haha* did it. And check out *mis sandalias,* my shoes, wise guy." Tony wiggled his big toes and danced so that the wooden sandals sounded against the sidewalk.

Lincoln introduced Tony to Mitsuo, who bowed. Tony bowed and then shook hands *raza*-style. Mitsuo

49

smiled and asked, "Please, shake hands again." They shook hands slowly, over and over, until Mitsuo pulled his hand away and muttered, "Interesting."

"Where you guys coming from?" Tony asked as they walked down the street together. "You look like Tom Sawyer and Huck Finn."

"We went fishing."

"Fishing? Where's the river? I don't see one." Always the joker, Tony shaded his eyes and looked skyward, then up and down the street. "There's a river in town?"

They crossed the street and moved into the shadows that hugged the storefronts. It was not much cooler there; it might even have been hotter among the hordes of shoppers. As they passed the *sentō*, Lincoln asked Tony, "You been here yet?"

"Aw, man, three times a day," Tony said. "*Hace mucho calor* in this *barrio*. I thought Japan was near the North Pole. How come it's so hot?"

"It just is," Mitsuo answered, shrugging.

The three of them stopped for bottles of Coca-Cola, which they drank while thumbing through comic books. Lincoln and Tony enjoyed the futuristic drawings.

Mitsuo asked Tony to come to his house for dinner, but Tony declined. "Thank you, but my folks expect me." Turning to Lincoln, he said, "Check this out, homes." He straightened his robe and stood straight up. "I'm an artist."

"What do you mean?"

"I mean, I'm an artist, a regular Picasso. My family makes statues of these holy dudes, and I'm helping them out."

"Dudes?"

"You know—saints or something."

Mitsuo said, "Buddhas."

"Yeah, that's the guy, and some other *vatos*."

"Lighten up, Tony. It's not cool to call them *vatos*. If they're saints."

Tony thought a moment. "I guess you're right. Anyways, I gotta go. See ya."

As Tony started to walk away, Lincoln pulled him aside, whispering, "You know what would be nice— if we could cook our *familias* Mexican food."

Tony snapped his fingers. "Good idea. I tried to explain *frijoles* and enchiladas to them, but they didn't get it."

"But we don't have any beans, or flour for tortillas."

"That's what you think." Tony grinned.

"You brought some?" Lincoln asked, eyebrows lifted.

"Sho 'nuff. Five-pound bag. You thought I was going to be in Japan six whole weeks and not grub on *frijoles?*"

Lincoln punched him in the arm. "You're my main man, Tony."

"How 'bout we meet at the *sentō* tomorrow. Four?"

"Sounds good."

"Catch you later."

Lincoln turned to Mitsuo, who had been watching them conspire.

Lincoln and Mitsuo started home, their fishing poles over their shoulders. It was not until they got to the gate of the farm that Mitsuo asked, "Are you mad at Tony?"

Lincoln furrowed his brow. "Mad?"

"Yes. You hit him in the arm."

"No way," Lincoln said, closing the gate behind him. "It's something you do." Lincoln thought for a moment, then said, "It's sorta like a bow. It means you like the person." Lincoln punched Mitsuo in the arm softly.

Mitsuo reflected on the punch, then said, "I like it."

AFTER DINNER, THE family sat on the *engawa*, catching the evening wind and eating ice cream. Mrs. Ono fanned herself with a magazine, cheeks flushed, strands of hair out of place. Mr. Ono, glasses on, read the newspaper, his empty bowl at his feet. He reported, "There was a fire in San Francisco, Lincoln-kun."

Lincoln looked over his shoulder, scraping the bottom of his bowl with his spoon. "Where?"

Mr. Ono pointed a thick finger at the story. "It says it was at an oil repository. Hunters Point."

Repository? Lincoln thought. What's that?

"Do you know Hunters Point?" asked Mr. Ono as he took off his glasses and wiped sweat from his brow.

"I've never been there. But I know it's near Candlestick Park."

Mr. Ono grunted and said, "San Francisco must be very, very big," and returned to reading his newspaper.

Lincoln turned to Mrs. Ono. "Will you please cut my hair? For *kempō*."

She looked at his long and straggly hair and asked Mitsuo in Japanese for the scissors. Mitsuo scurried into the house and came out with a wooden box.

"*Dōzo*. Please come," she said to Lincoln, rising.

In the yard, in the glow of the porch light, Lincoln sat with a dishcloth wrapped around his shoulders.

"You'll look different," Mitsuo commented, eating a juicy peach. He licked his fingers and wiped his hands on his pants. "You'll look like me." He raked his hand over his shaved head.

Mrs. Ono worked quickly, the cold scissors snaking around Lincoln's ears. Then she ran a clipperlike scissor over the top of his head. The hair piled onto the towel, and some strands drifted to the ground, where the cat batted at them. Lincoln's long locks were gone. In their place were bristles that tickled his palm.

Lincoln rose from the chair and brushed the hair off his shoulders.

"I am not finished," Mrs. Ono said. She spoke to Mitsuo in Japanese, and he went inside.

Lincoln's eyes grew big when Mitsuo returned with a smooth, foot-long stick. "What's that?" It looked like some sort of doctor's tool and reminded Lincoln of every injection he had had at Kaiser Hospital.

"A *mimikaki*. An ear pick. It will not hurt," Mrs.

Ono said, prodding him up to the *engawa*. She sat down and patted her lap. "Put your head here."

"My head!" Lincoln felt embarrassed; no one had ever cleaned his ears. He looked at Mitsuo for help, but Mitsuo was eating another peach and holding back a sticky smile. "It's painless," he said. "Easy."

Lincoln narrowed his eyes in distrust. When he was five he had stuck a match inside his ear, and the match snapped off. He didn't tell his mother for three days, not until he had lost most of his hearing in that ear and went around yelling "Huh?" whenever his mother spoke to him. Even the doctor had had a difficult time getting the match out.

"It feels good. I'll show you." Mitsuo snuggled his head onto his mother's lap and closed his eyes as she probed his right ear. Now and then she pulled out a clot of wax and wiped it onto a paper towel.

After both ears were cleaned, Mitsuo jumped to his feet. "See?" He cupped a hand around his ear. "I can hear better."

Knowing that he had no choice, Lincoln laid his head in Mrs. Ono's lap. He winced as the ear pick probed in slow circles. But as Mitsuo had said, it felt good. He almost fell asleep.

Mrs. Ono laughed and wiped the *mimikaki* on the towel. "Lots of lumps," she said.

Lincoln laughed to hide his embarrassment. He promised himself that he would clean his ears more carefully from that day on.

THAT NIGHT AT *kempō*, he felt strong. Dressed in his *gi*, he stretched between two black belts on the lawn. He did fifty push-ups and a hundred sit-ups, and he jumped to his feet, breathing hard. He ran his hand over his head. Smooth was his favorite feeling.

They practiced throws during the intense workout. Lincoln was tossed repeatedly, coming down each time like a cat. He had seen his *sensei* in San Francisco come down on both feet, his hands up and ready to fight. Now *he* was doing it, and he felt like he could take on the world—or at least his neighborhood back in San Francisco.

Oyama-*sensei* had been studying Lincoln's technique from a distance. She stepped in between Lincoln and another brown belt, both of whom were breathing hard.

"Like this," she explained, gripping Lincoln's *gi* as she pivoted her hip onto his. She pulled Lincoln off balance and tossed him into the air. He came down halfway across the yard, on his knees, with one hand in the pond and the other in the mud. He shook the mud off his hands and, looking up, said, "Wow!"

"Sorry, Lincoln-kun," Oyama-*sensei* said. "Are you OK?"

Lincoln shrugged it off. "I'm fine."

That night he hobbled home, a spark of pain in his back.

———

THE NEXT DAY, after Lincoln and Mitsuo had worked only a few hours in the field, Mitsuo's mother said,

"Go and have a drink." She pressed yen into their hands.

The boys hurried into town for a soda. In a far corner of the ice-cream parlor, two old men sat under an overhead fan playing *go*. Lincoln and Mitsuo drank their sodas quickly, ordered seconds, and watched the men, neither of whom seemed to notice the boys. The men sat quietly, and thoughtfully rubbed their whiskered chins as they considered the next strategy.

Lincoln and Mitsuo were wandering around town again when Mitsuo said, "Let me show you something very interesting." He led Lincoln down a narrow alley filled with smoke. The ring of iron on iron sounded in the air, and flames could be seen flashing in a work shed.

"My uncle is a master sword maker," Mitsuo said, a hint of pride in his voice.

Lincoln's curiosity grew as he peeked inside the shed and saw a young man turning a length of metal over an open fire.

"Is that your uncle?" Lincoln asked.

"No, that's an apprentice." Mitsuo spoke to the young man in Japanese. The apprentice pointed to another room and returned to work.

For a few minutes Lincoln and Mitsuo watched the apprentice roll the crude sword over the fire, then dip it into water mixed with ash. A gray cloud puffed up and drifted toward the darkened ceiling.

The uncle appeared from the other room, tying his hair back with a *hachimaki*, a headband. His skin was dark, his arms splotched from burns, and his

57

clothes black with soot. His eyeglasses were flecked with ash.

"Mitsuo-kun, what brings you here?" he asked in Japanese.

Mitsuo bowed deeply to his uncle and introduced Lincoln, who bowed in turn and said, "*Ohayō gozaimasu.*"

"*Ohayō,*" the uncle greeted them. He apologized that he didn't have anything for them to drink. He offered them a stick of gum, and they accepted politely with bows of thanks, though each of them already had a pack of gum.

"We were just passing," Mitsuo said. "Lincoln is staying with us for the summer. He's from California."

"Ah, so. California." He beamed, turning to Lincoln. Mitsuo translated for his uncle, who said that his best customers were from California.

Lincoln smiled but didn't say anything. He was in awe of the master swordsmith. He was in awe of Japan. He had already met two honest-to-goodness masters—first in *kempō* and now in sword making.

Mitsuo's uncle talked, hands pressed together, and Mitsuo translated, "Uncle asks if there are millionaires on every street in California. That's what he hears."

"Not on my street," Lincoln replied. He thought of his old neighborhood in the Mission District, where junky cars often sat on blocks and litter scuttled freely when the wind picked up. If there were a millionaire, it would probably be the liquor-store owner, who did

58

a brisk business at five when the workers got off from the warehouse near Valencia Street.

Lincoln and Mitsuo stayed awhile. They watched the length of metal as it was heated over the fire. The apprentice rolled it through the flames, pounded it over an anvil, and heated it again until it glowed neon orange.

"It's bad," Lincoln said in praise.

"Yes, very, very bad," Mitsuo repeated.

From the sword foundry, Lincoln and Mitsuo returned home. While they played catch in the yard, Mitsuo lamented the fact that he hadn't made the summer baseball league.

"That's a drag," Lincoln said as he picked up an easy grounder and sidearmed it to Mitsuo.

"A 'drag'?" Mitsuo asked. "What do you mean?"

Lincoln explained, and after much thought, Mitsuo remarked, "Very American."

"Americans talk in slang. There is Mexican slang, black slang, Asian slang, yuppie slang."

Mitsuo sighed and said, "I'll never learn English. It is too difficult."

"You will. When you come to see me in San Francisco, you'll be rattlin' your lips like the rest of us."

When it was close to four, Lincoln told Mitsuo that he had to meet Tony.

"I'll come," Mitsuo said, tossing his glove onto the porch and scaring the cat.

"No," Lincoln said. He and Tony were going to plan the party for their host families and it had to be a surprise.

Mitsuo looked hurt; Lincoln tried to explain that they were meeting to plan something special. "It's a surprise," Lincoln said. "You'll see."

"A surprise?"

"Yes. A surprise."

"Don't get lost." Mitsuo walked Lincoln to the gate. He pointed down the street and told him three times to take a left and go right at the first signal. Lincoln turned around when he was halfway down the street and saw Mitsuo at the gate, pointing right.

That *vato* is all right, Lincoln said to himself. He felt bad leaving Mitsuo at home. I should have invited him, he told himself. As punishment, he punched a wall and hurt his hand.

Lincoln found Tony already undressed. An old man was scrubbing his back, muttering something in Japanese.

"Hey, Linc," Tony greeted him.

"Who's the guy?" Lincoln asked.

"I don't know. He just started scrubbing my back."

Lincoln undressed as he watched Tony trade places and scrub the man's back. The man scolded in Japanese, and although neither Lincoln nor Tony could understand the words, both knew that the man wanted to be scrubbed hard. Lincoln grabbed a washcloth and helped Tony rub the man's back. When they finished, the man stood up, bowed, and got into the pool, sighing loudly.

Lincoln and Tony planned the party as they sat in the tub.

"How 'bout Friday?" Tony asked.

"Sounds good. Do you know how to make tortillas?"

"No. I thought you did."

"Not really. But I've watched my mom a million times." Lincoln fanned his face. "Man, you could kill someone with this water."

"Tell you what, Linc. I brought the beans. Why don't I give them to you and let you cook them?"

"You brought the beans?"

"Yeah." Tony pointed to his backpack, which was in the wicker basket.

"Fair enough, if you make the tortillas." Lincoln rose from the water and toweled off. "See if you can find some avocados. I'll look for chilies and tomatoes, and make some salsa. Let's meet here again tomorrow."

They dressed and started home, stopping to drink Cokes and thumb through comic books at a newsstand.

Lincoln said, "Let me try some Japanese on you." He thought deeply and then said, "*Anata no tan'joobi wa itsu desu ka?*"

"Whatta you say?" Tony asked.

"I think, 'What day is your birthday?' or 'What is your favorite color?' I forget which. Mitsuo was trying to teach me."

"Today's my birthday," Tony cracked, "and money's my favorite color. *¿Entiendes?*"

Lincoln punched his friend in the arm and headed home.

9

THE NEXT MORNING, after breakfast, Mrs. Ono asked
Lincoln and Mitsuo to work in a neighbor's field. The
neighbor was too old to tend the crop of green beans
herself; her husband, a distant relative of Mrs. Ono's,
had passed away the spring before. When Mitsuo protested that he and Lincoln had planned to play baseball
that morning, Mrs. Ono scolded him.

"She is old. You must help her."

"Why us?" Mitsuo pleaded. His baseball mitt
hung from the end of his arm.

"Because you must."

"Doesn't she have relatives?"

"We are her relatives. Now, please, do not argue.
Someday when you are old, you will see."

So the boys shouldered their hoes and walked to the neighbor's garden. The weeds were as tall as car antennas, and gnats swarmed around the fruit the peach tree had dropped.

Lincoln and Mitsuo looked at each other.

"This is going to be a lot of work," Lincoln said, rolling up his shirt sleeves. He tried to convince himself that it would make him stronger for kempō. Whacking at the weeds would pump blood to his arms and legs.

"We may die before the day is over," Mitsuo said as he unbuttoned his shirt and let it hang open. He shaded his eyes with his hand and looked toward the blazing sun.

Mrs. Nakayama, a wizened woman with only a few teeth and a face puckered with wrinkles, came out to the back porch and greeted them. Mitsuo and Lincoln each gave a short, polite bow.

Bowing in return, she thanked them for coming—and then told them to get to work. She sat in the shade of the porch and banged her cane, scaring up a puff of dust.

Without a word, Lincoln and Mitsuo started hoeing fiercely, the weeds falling like timber as they advanced up the first row. Maps of sweat spread on the backs of their shirts. Sweat dripped from the end of Lincoln's nose. Sweat rolled into his ears. He saw a large bead of sweat hanging on the end of Mitsuo's nose as well. It dropped on a leaf, like rain, and another bead formed.

Mitsuo looked at the woman, whose cat lay sleeping in her lap. "My mother says she's a relative of ours, but I doubt it."

Lincoln wiped his face with his shirt sleeve and blinked away a crust of dirt from his eyelashes. He thought about the neighbor in San Francisco for whom he had mowed the lawn for three quarters and a bagful of crushed aluminum cans. That woman was so cheap she couldn't even offer Lincoln a smile.

He stood up, leaning on his hoe to give himself a rest. "You know, Mitsuo, the farms in California are sometimes a thousand acres—or even bigger."

Mitsuo squinted a doubtful eye at Lincoln. "Really?"

"Yeah. I know they're small here, but whenever we drive through the San Joaquin Valley, the farms go on for miles. But they don't belong to everybody, just to big growers."

"I would like to see this," Mitsuo said.

"You will. When you come and visit us."

The sun moved slowly overhead. Flies buzzed past their ears like fighter jets. Some of the gnats left the rotting peaches and hovered around their faces.

"This is gross," Lincoln said. He smacked his neck and three bloody gnats lay squashed in his palm. He washed his hand in a puddle of muddy water.

Mitsuo cursed in Japanese and apologized. "See what I mean," he said. "We just work and never play."

"Yeah." Lincoln grunted as he raised a bucket of water onto his shoulder. "Maybe we should sneak away."

"Sneak away! My father would kill me, and you too. We must respect our elders. We have to stay."

Lincoln staggered to the row and splashed the water among the green beans. "How come she don't have a garden hose?" he asked.

"She works the old way."

"But she's not doing the work. We are!"

Three hours later they finally finished working. Mitsuo poured a bucket of cold water over Lincoln, and Lincoln poured one over Mitsuo.

The old neighbor climbed down the steps to inspect their work. She pointed to weeds they had missed.

"We can't please her," Lincoln hissed as he plucked the last weeds.

Mitsuo said, "Let's go."

"Yeah, let's blow this place."

"What is the meaning of 'blow this place'?"

"It means 'let's leave'—*adios!*"

The old neighbor called them back and shook a paper bag at them.

"*¡Ay, caramba!* What does the *vieja* want *now?*" Lincoln asked. "Do we have to take out her garbage?"

They turned and walked back. Mitsuo bowed and accepted the bag. Only when they were down the street and happy to be free did they open it. They found bruised peaches, which gave off a strong fruity odor and a horde of gnats that rose from the bag like smoke.

Mitsuo splattered the peaches, one by one, against a wall.

"Rotten luck, rotten peaches," Lincoln said. "Hey, that's pretty good. I'm doin' rap."

BACK HOME, THEY joined the cat and fell asleep on the porch. They woke when Mr. Ono came home, nudged Mitsuo in the rib with his foot, and said, "Let us eat."

They staggered to the bathroom and scrubbed their faces and arms before joining Mitsuo's father and mother at the table. A letter lay next to Lincoln's placemat.

"A letter from my mom!" Lincoln smiled.

Mr. Ono, his cheek fat with rice, said, "Let us hear, Lincoln-kun."

"Yes, please," Mrs. Ono said as she poured tea for her husband.

Lincoln tore open the letter. He was occasionally homesick, especially at night, when he would lie in bed and think about his mother. He missed her. He missed his own bedroom and the familiar streets of San Francisco. And he was anxious to hear if his dog, Flaco, was OK. Before he'd left for Japan, Flaco had gotten into a fight with an alley cat who had dug her claws into Flaco's nose. Lincoln began to read silently:

Dear *Mi'jo,*

I miss you very much. I hope you and Tony are behaving and not goofing around. I don't want your host family to think you're a low-class *chango.* Do you hear me? I miss you very much, but how come you didn't tell me where you left the key to the back door? Nothing is really happening around here, except that that stupid Maxima is in the shop, and it's going to cost nearly a thousand dollars to fix. It's a piece of junk after all. And your crazy dog brought a dead sparrow into the house. I could've killed him. His nose is better. . . .

Lincoln swallowed a mouthful of rice and wondered how he could share this letter. He didn't want the Onos to think that his mother was mean or anything. So he read aloud his own version:

"My dearest Lincoln,

I miss you very much. I am lonely and in need of your excellent help. It seems that I damaged the Maxima when I braked too hard. Now the brakes are stuck. I know that you could fix them if you were here. You have a mechanical mind. You are as smart as any boy in all of San Francisco, and maybe the whole West. I miss you very much. You are my only son, and sweet Tony is like a son, too. I know you two boys are bringing Mexican pride to Japan."

Lincoln read a few more made-up sentences, then folded the letter and placed it in his shirt pocket next to his heart.

"Nice mother," Mrs. Ono said, her eyes shining with affection. "One day we would like to meet her."

"You will," Lincoln said. "When you come to San Francisco."

Mr. Ono put down his chopsticks and said reflectively, "A thoughtful mother." With his hands resting in his lap he began to tell a story about his grandmother, who used to write weekly letters to her son, Mr. Ono's father.

Mr. Ono explained that the war had just broken out. His grandparents and their family were living in Hiroshima. For more than four generations they had been carpenters, but the war changed that. The men were sent to fight, and women, even mothers, were forced to work in factories. Seeing that a large city in wartime was no place for children, his grandparents had decided to move their children—including Mr. Ono's father—to the countryside, where they would wait out the war on an uncle's farm.

"Was this World War Two?" Lincoln asked.

"Yes. It was long ago. It was a terrible time for our country. The world. I was not born then, not until after the war. But I know my parents and grandparents had very little to eat, almost nothing. Not like this." He tapped his bowl of rice with his chopstick. Lincoln and Mitsuo stopped eating to listen. "My father told me that he received a letter from his mother every week. She was still living in the city. She was working in a tire factory. It was very sad for my father."

Mr. Ono said the letters were like poetry. "She would write my father little songs, which he and his brothers sang. Clapped and sang. Sometimes she would slip a piece of gum into the letters. He liked

68

that. All the brothers had to share it, but still, a little sweetness went a long way." He took a sip of tea and continued, "My great uncle—Uncle Kaz—was a fine man. He grew apples, and my father helped him as much as he could. Poor Father, he missed his mother. He was eleven years old then."

"He must have been happy to see her when the war was over," Lincoln said. He took a sip of his tea, which was now cold.

Mr. Ono's face darkened. Mitsuo and Mrs. Ono grew quiet, and Lincoln put down his cup.

"He did not see her. The letters stopped. Everything stopped," Mr. Ono said. "She worked three years in the tire factory, and then—"

Mother and son looked down at their food. They knew this story.

The house was so quiet Lincoln could hear the kitchen faucet dripping like tears. The wooden floor creaked. The neighbor's dog barked. Lincoln studied his hands, which were rough from work and *kempō*.

Mr. Ono said softly, "Lincoln-kun, it is not your fault, but your country dropped the atomic bomb on Hiroshima."

Lincoln felt awful. In his mind, he saw a flash of silvery light fill the sky and a mushroom cloud unfold. He saw families crying and tongues of flames wagging from charred buildings.

Before Lincoln could say anything, Mr. Ono smiled at him and said, "That is why you are here. You are an American boy. As an exchange student, you share yourself with us." He lifted his chopsticks

69

and clicked them together as he raised his bowl. "Let us eat. No food should be wasted."

The family took up their bowls, filled them with new, hot rice, and ate. After dinner Lincoln volunteered to wash the dishes. He scrubbed the pots with vigor, mad at himself for ever thinking that war movies were fun.

After the dishes were done, Lincoln left for *kempō*, his *gi* over his shoulder. He was disturbed that Mr. Ono had grown up without knowing his grandmother, and that she had died so terribly. Lincoln felt the need to work out hard, to feel real pain. That night he was thrown into the air more than a dozen times, sometimes coming down on his feet like a cat. More often than not, he came down on his back. The wind was knocked out of him each time, and twice he felt his bones crack. He wished he could hurt even more, but the cushion of spongy grass saved him from any serious injury.

Before he left, Oyama-*sensei* called him aside.

"Lincoln-kun," she said quietly. "Please come and see me tomorrow. At twelve."

"OK," Lincoln said. He wondered why but held his tongue. He *gasshō*-ed, saluted, and raced home under the star-flecked sky. He thought that Oyama-*sensei* might want to teach him a new technique, one that would fend off even the baddest of bad dudes.

10

"NINETY-SEVEN, NINETY-eight, ninety-nine, one hundred." Lincoln grunted as he finished a set of a hundred push-ups, and collapsed so exhausted that his arms twitched. He was still tired from yesterday's hard *kempō* workout. His face pressed to the porch, he saw an ant stagger past, carrying a grain of rice. He remembered reading somewhere that for their size ants were about the strongest creatures on earth. Lincoln blew at the ant and sent it sailing.

"OK, my turn," Mitsuo said. He readied for his last set of push-ups and started counting. "*Ichi, ni, san, shi . . .*"

Mrs. Ono called from the house. "Lincoln-kun," she said. "It is your mother on the telephone."

Lincoln grinned and jumped to his feet. He wagged a playfully threatening finger at Mitsuo. "You better play fair. Don't slack off."

"I promise," Mitsuo grunted, holding back a mischievous smile.

Lincoln took the call in the living room. "Hi, Mom. How's everything?"

"Hi, *mi'jo*," said the crackling voice on the other end. "Fine. Roy and I just got back from dinner and a movie."

"It's night there?"

"Yes, it's really late."

"That's funny. It's morning over here," Lincoln said. "What did you have for dinner?"

"Japanese food. In honor of you."

"That's funny, so did we."

Mrs. Mendoza asked Lincoln if he was eating enough vegetables, getting enough meat, and drinking enough milk.

"Lots," he lied. He had eaten more vegetables in one week in Japan than he did in one year in California, and so much spinach that he felt like Popeye. But he had eaten almost no meat and had drunk only a few swallows of milk. The Onos, like most Japanese families, preferred seafood and tea to meat and milk.

"How's Flaco?" Lincoln asked.

"*Está bien*," she answered. "He got in another fight with that cat, but I think he won this time. He had some cat fur between his teeth."

"The stud," Lincoln crowed. "Give him a dog biscuit for me."

By the time they said good-bye, his mother's voice was cracking.

"Drink all your milk," his mother sobbed. "I'll see you in a few weeks. I miss you. *Adios.*"

As Lincoln hung up, he felt a lump in his throat. He missed his mother, and he missed Flaco, his best friend on shaggy fours.

Outside, he found Mitsuo in push-up position, counting, "a thousand three, a thousand four, a thousand five . . ."

"You liar," Lincoln growled, and pushed Mitsuo over with his foot.

"Really," Mitsuo pleaded, laughing. "I did a thousand. Look at all this sweat."

Lincoln looked at the small puddles and thought for a moment that maybe, just maybe, Mitsuo had actually done a thousand push-ups. Then Lincoln spied the garden hose lying nearby. "You think I was born yesterday?" Lincoln scowled, pointing to the hose. "Let's go. Oyama-*sensei* wants to talk to me."

"About what?"

Lincoln shrugged, his shoulders sore from the push-ups. "I don't know," he said. "Maybe she's gonna teach me a death blow or something."

When they arrived, Oyama was on her porch, sipping tea. She worked at home as a translator of medical dictionaries. Her languages were French and English, and she knew some Spanish.

Lincoln and Mitsuo bowed deeply, then climbed the steps and gave a second slight bow. Oyama gestured for them to join her. They plopped down, folding their legs underneath them. Lincoln looked around the yard. The grass was wild along the fence, and there was a green pond in the middle of the yard. A rusty bicycle leaned against a tree.

"Lincoln-kun, I need your help," Oyama began solemnly, rattling a sheaf of papers at Lincoln. "These are poems by a Japanese poet that I am translating into English. I would like you to read them carefully and suggest changes. My English is good, but yours, I feel, is better."

"Poems?" Lincoln asked. "I don't know how to spell good."

"They have nothing to do with spelling. Now please, take them home and read them carefully. If you think my language is wrong, please circle." She handed him the papers.

Lincoln and Mitsuo stared at the poems and read the start of one:

> *Overcast for days, and the gull circles*
> *This place of sleep. The shadows gobble*
> *The birds. I'm fifty-seven,*
> *My sled of years riding on my back.*

"Sounds all right to me," Lincoln said. "Except 'gobble.' That sounds weird. It reminds me of Thanksgiving."

"Good, Lincoln-kun. This is exactly what I'm looking for." Oyama beamed. "Please read the poems, and if the words are wrong, please tell me."

Oyama rose, her empty teacup in her hand, and

74

Lincoln and Mitsuo scrambled to their feet. "I will see you tonight," she said. She bowed and went inside.

The boys gathered the poems and went to get a soda. They took their drinks to a small park not too far from a shrine where passersby were bowing, lighting incense, and praying.

"Do you believe in God?" Lincoln asked.

"Yes. I believe if we make a mistake, God corrects us," Mitsuo said. He finished his drink and spun the bottle.

"I'm Catholic," Lincoln said. "When we make mistakes, we say confession."

"What's 'confession'?"

Lincoln took a swallow of his soda and answered, "It's when you go into a box in church and tell the priest what you did wrong. This way Jesus Christ forgives our sins, and we can start over."

"Box?"

"Well, not exactly a box. It's sort of like a closet. You're supposed to say your sins in private."

Mitsuo searched Lincoln's face and then asked, "Have you sinned?"

"Not really. I stole some things—gum and pumpkin seeds, and one time this." He tapped his soda bottle. "And once I took some glow-in-the-dark shoelaces from Woolworth—Woolworth is a store. I got caught. Mom lashed me good. Even my dog, Flaco, cried with me."

"We're Buddhist," Mitsuo said. "Almost all Japanese are Buddhist, but not many go to temple."

"What is Buddhist?" Lincoln asked.

"It's hard to explain. We worship Buddha. He's like your Jesus Christ."

Lincoln suddenly remembered that he had to meet Tony at the *sentō* at four so they could finish planning the Mexican dinner. He was already ten minutes late.

"Mitsuo, I got to tell you. Tony and I are planning a party for our families."

"A party?"

"Yeah, with Mexican food."

"Mexican food? How is food from Mexico?"

As they hurried up the street, Lincoln described enchiladas and tacos, piping-hot *frijoles* in a black pan, and steaming rice. He told of tortillas made of corn and flour, and wrapped in dish towels. He praised the fiery salsa of his *tío* Junior, and tamales on Christmas Day at his *tía* Linda's. And he told about eating with tortillas, not forks or spoons or chopsticks, and said there was nothing better than scraping a small rip of tortilla across a puddle of chicken *mole*.

"Sounds good," Mitsuo remarked.

"It is. *Es muy rico.*"

At the *sentō*, Tony was neck deep in hot water. He whistled at Lincoln and Mitsuo. Soon their three heads bobbed on the surface of the water.

They talked food that afternoon, their mouths watering for a pile of cheese-laced *frijoles*.

11

MR. ONO RAISED his dinner plate to his face and studied the puddle of steaming *frijoles* curiously. His nostrils sniffed its aroma. "I know this smell," he said as he raked a chopstick across the plate and sucked on the end. He closed his eyes and smiled as the steam rose from the dish.

"I know this taste," he concluded, opening his eyes and nodding his head in approval.

"How can you know?" Mrs. Ono said.

"I just *know*," he answered.

Mrs. Ono looked at their guests, the Inabas, and raised her glass of beer in salute to them. They, in turn, saluted the Onos. She took a tiny, birdlike sip and said, "My husband thinks that he likes foreign food. He just likes noodles and fish. He is not very adventurous."

"I like all kinds of food," Mr. Ono argued.

"Noodles and fish," Mrs. Ono countered playfully.

"No, I am an international eater. Don't you recall the time I tried snake when I was in Thailand? I tried it, but I felt guilty because sometimes I feel slippery as a snake. How could I eat my own kind?" He laughed at his joke and took a drink of his beer, smacking his lips.

Mrs. Ono rolled her eyes and got up to check on the boys in the kitchen. For the past three hours, Lincoln and Tony had been preparing the food. They'd cooked the beans and smashed them into *frijoles;* they'd chopped chilies, onions, and tomatoes for salsa; they'd squeezed dough and rolled it into odd-shaped tortillas; they'd cooked ground beef. Now they brought the rest of the food to the table and joined their families.

"We are honored that you invited us," Mr. Inaba said to the Onos, smiling so that the gold crowns on his teeth showed. "We have heard so much about your family."

"We have heard about your family as well," Mrs. Ono said.

Mrs. Inaba looked at Tony. "Tony-kun is a hard-working boy."

Tony raised his hands and showed them his dime-sized blisters. Along with the Inabas' son, Toshi, he had worked their patch of cabbages and radishes into healthy vegetables they would later sell on the roadside.

"He also taught our son valuable American words."

"Such as?" Mr. Ono asked, trying some more *frijoles*.

Mr. Inaba thought and then said, "*Órale, ése.*" He turned to Tony, who was headed back to the kitchen to fry more tortillas, and yelled, "*¡Órale, ése!*"

"*Simón que sí, Papi,*" Tony called back as he turned over one of his homemade tortillas. The tortilla puffed up like a blimp. Tony stabbed it with a fork and the hot air sighed out.

"Lincoln is nice boy, too," Mrs. Ono volunteered. "He is practicing *kempō.*"

"*Kempō?*" Mr. Inaba looked at Lincoln, sizing him up, and asked, "Who is your teacher?"

"Oyama-*sensei,*" Lincoln said. "She's bad."

" 'Bad'?" repeated Mr. Inaba. "But I thought she was an excellent teacher."

" 'Bad' means good," Mrs. Ono said. "It is an American expression. Very valuable word."

Tony returned from the kitchen with a dish towel of warm tortillas. "Here, try another before they get cold."

Lincoln took the dish towel from Tony and offered the stack of tortillas to Mr. Inaba, who was sampling his *frijoles.* When Mr. Inaba bit into a tortilla, it crackled like a Dorito. He grunted and commented, "Interesting food."

Lincoln looked at Tony, and Tony looked back.

Lincoln muttered, "We messed up. These tortillas are hard as rocks."

"Harder," Tony whispered back. "And the avocados ain't any good either. Five bucks apiece, man, and they're mostly black as the soul of my cousin Pete. And the dude's in jail."

"No wonder you two are so strong," Mrs. Inaba said, attempting a compliment. "The food is so hard." Even the *frijoles* were undercooked, so they had to mash them with their teeth before they could swallow. They washed them down with tea or beer. The salsa was more like ketchup than the fiery sauce that Lincoln's and Tony's mothers concocted every Saturday morning. But the families tried it all, smiled between bites, drank their beer and tea, and made small talk about the weather, the traffic, and the new emperor.

After dinner the four boys went to Mitsuo's room, where they played Nintendo and ate *nigirimeshi*, rice balls, because they were still hungry. Tony and Lincoln punched each other in the arm.

"We messed up," Tony said, a grain of rice clinging to his chin.

"You've got rice on your face," Lincoln said. He turned to the Japanese boys. "Mexican food *really* is good. If we knew how to cook, you'd die in paradise. My mom makes the best enchiladas."

"We believe you," said Toshi. "If we had to make Japanese food, we would make it terrible also."

"I'm sure you guys could do better," Tony said.

"No, we would starve," Mitsuo said. Toshi nodded in agreement.

Mitsuo suggested that they go and get ice-cream cones. They left through the window, stepping carefully over the garden for fear that they would trample a tomato. Then they would really be in trouble.

———

WHEN THEY SAW that they had been gone nearly an hour, they raced home, knots of hunger twisting in their stomachs. And they arrived just in time: the adults were frying a fish that was nearly as large as a guitar. A new pot of rice was steaming. The tea was simmering, and icy bottles of *ramune* were waiting. Then, at a quarter to ten, with the moon hanging like a sickle in the sky, the fiesta really began.

12

MR. ONO PACKED the car with borrowed camping gear. He had a week of vacation, and he planned to spend a few days in the forest with Lincoln and Mitsuo. They would bike up a path where Buddhist worshipers went to pray at shrines and pay homage to dead ancestors. Mrs. Ono would stay home, enjoying a vacation from the three of them and their incessant need for food.

Lincoln was free to go because he had returned the poems to Oyama-*sensei*, marked up with changes. He had been glad to get them out of the way. His own writing was terrible, and the thought of helping someone write poems scared him to death. As parting advice, Oyama-*sensei* had told him to practice *kempō* while he was away because soon after he returned he would have to take his second *kyu* test.

"It is good to get away," Mr. Ono said as he stuffed the backpacks and feather-light tent into the trunk of the car. "Tall trees. Silence. Peace."

Lincoln enjoyed camping. Once he had spent four days in Yosemite hiking in the snow with two uncles. He had thought he would freeze stiff as a root-beer Popsicle, but actually he had been hot most of the time, because hiking in the snow was tiring. His mother frowned at the idea of camping. She liked to sleep in a bed, not on the ground. She was scared that a raccoon might bite her while she slept, or that a spider might climb into her ear and hatch eggs that would make their way into a gray fold in her brain.

Mr. Ono and the boys drove for three hours, until they came to a mountain. Then the car began to climb and the air thinned. When they rolled down the windows, the air rushed into their lungs so Lincoln and Mitsuo had difficulty breathing. When they took a corner, their chewing gum flew from their mouths. At this they laughed so hard that Mr. Ono growled and told them to shut up because they were disturbing nature.

When they arrived at the foot of the trail, Mitsuo and Lincoln were nearly carsick. The last six miles had been twists and turns. At five thousand feet, the towns had given way to acres of trees.

"I got a frog in my stomach," Lincoln groaned.

"A frog?" Mitsuo asked.

"I feel like I'm going to throw up my breakfast."

"I suggest that you do not," Mr. Ono said, heaving the backpacks onto the ground. "From now on we eat once a day. Only *nigirimeshi*."

"Only rice balls?" Lincoln asked, leaning against the car.

"Rice and tea. We are here on a pilgrimage."

The path started out wide as a city street but soon narrowed into a trail of pine needles and dank earth. They walked single file, silent. Lincoln's nausea had left him, and now he was hungry. He thought, Rice and tea. Rice and tea. The pine needles crunched under the soles of his shoes; with each crunch he pictured a bowl of Shredded Wheat, his least-favorite cereal. Right now it didn't sound so bad.

After an hour they rested on a fallen tree that was green with moss. A shred of blue sky showed between the tall pines. In the distance, they could hear a river rushing over rocks.

"This feels good," Mr. Ono said as he peeled off his gloves.

Mitsuo whispered to Lincoln, "Are you hungry?"

Lincoln licked his lips and pressed the heel of his palm into his cavernous stomach. "I could eat a horse."

"A horse?" Mitsuo asked. "Do Americans eat horses?"

"It's an expression, Mitsuo. But I *could* eat a small pig. Between slices of bread." The boys laughed at the image of a whole pig laid out between huge slices of bread.

"On a pilgrimage, we go hungry," Mr. Ono said.

"In a little while you will see a shrine and maybe a priest praying. Maybe other people like us."

They were four miles into the forest and hadn't seen any other hikers.

"Where is everyone?" Lincoln asked.

"It's the wrong season," Mitsuo said. "Most come in October, not July. We are lucky that few people are around. Usually it is crowded."

"I wouldn't mind seeing some people. What if something happened to us?"

"Yeah, we could starve. I don't know why my father is not letting us eat."

After a few swallows of water from their canteens, they started again. Lincoln's backpack felt as heavy as his cousins used to when he would give them piggyback rides around the front yard. Although the late-afternoon air was chilly, he was sweating.

They soon came upon a shrine, where a stone statue wore a woven hat and sat under a wooden shelter. A stalk of incense sent up a feathery, sweet-smelling smoke that the wind broke apart.

"This is the *Jizō*. He watches over children," Mr. Ono said to Lincoln. "He protects you, and you, too, Mitsuo."

Hands pressed together in prayer, he bowed toward the shrine. Mitsuo and Lincoln bowed with their eyes closed.

"There's a Catholic saint who protects children, but I forgot his name," Lincoln said. You should have paid more attention in catechism, he scolded himself.

And what if I need to call on this saint? How would I ask? Please, Saint What's-Your-Name—help me!

"*Jizō* means 'womb,' " Mr. Ono said, touching the statue's belly. "He gives you comfort. We will see him many times on our trip."

They took a few swallows of water and continued their trek. It was nearly dark. They walked three more miles, then pitched a tent among the ferns.

"Feels good," Mitsuo said, unlacing his boots.

Lincoln cracked the knuckles of his toes. "I'm hurting."

"Could you eat a horse?" Mitsuo asked.

"If I had enough mustard, I could eat it alive."

But there were no horses to eat for dinner. They each ate two rice balls, washing them down with cold tea. After this Mr. Ono whittled a stick, and Lincoln and Mitsuo talked awhile, mostly about baseball and girls, arguing whether girls were more beautiful with long or short hair. Then they climbed into their sleeping bags. Lincoln felt sticky but good. His stomach growled, but he didn't care. This was the fifth time he had gone camping, and the first in a foreign country. Now if only he could dream in Japanese.

———

LINCOLN WOKE IN the morning stiff as a twig. He was hurting from the long walk and the hard earth, earth that had looked so soft when they pitched the tent. He stretched and let out a sleepy yawn. One of his socks had worked its way off his foot. He plunged a groping hand to the end of the sleeping bag and fetched it. He then nudged Mitsuo and said, "Get up, man."

Mitsuo let out a small moan but didn't stir.

Lincoln pulled back the flap of the tent and crawled out. Mr. Ono, unshaven, was rubbing his hands over a small fire. He said, "*Ohayō!* Good morning, Lincoln-kun."

"*Ohayō*," Lincoln said as he pulled himself to his feet. He did a few squats to get the blood going, then joined Mr. Ono for tea.

"Smell the trees," Mr. Ono said. He stretched, sucked in some fresh air, and let it out in a long sigh. "Hm—my arm has some pain. Right here." He touched his shoulder.

Lincoln splashed water from a metal pot onto his sleepy face. "Maybe you slept wrong," he said, shuddering from the cold. "I slept on my shoe." He rubbed his back where the shoe had poked him all night.

"No, this is different." Mr. Ono peeled off his jacket and shirt, and probed his arm. When he saw two red, swollen points, he looked serious.

"So this is it," he said calmly. "They look like spider bites." He pinched the bites until a clear pus ran like tears.

"It's ugly," Lincoln said, now fully awake. He had awakened hungry, but now his hunger collapsed to nothing. "Does it hurt?"

"No. What spider can hurt an old man like me?"

Mitsuo surfaced from the tent and asked, "What's going on?"

"A spider bit your dad," Lincoln said.

"It is nothing," Mr. Ono said. He handed cups of steaming tea to the boys and shrugged back into his shirt.

"Let me see," Mitsuo asked.

"It is nothing. I get hurt at work all the time. Now hurry up and let us get ready to go." He buttoned his shirt and slipped his jacket back on.

Lincoln had been bitten countless times. Once by a parrot, twice by a dog, six times by a cat, and every summer for fourteen years by a zillion blood-sucking mosquitoes. And once he had been bitten by a baby cousin. Luckily, the baby was toothless; it only took a tickle under her chin to relax her jaws.

To get his blood going, Lincoln practiced prearranged *kempō* forms. Mitsuo followed along, laughing because he couldn't do them right.

"You're not helping," Lincoln scolded. "Be serious. I'm going to test in two weeks."

After their breakfast of rice balls and tea, they broke camp and continued on their journey. They walked in a line between the shadows of the tall trees, with Lincoln last. The ferns unfolded like large green waves, and moss gripped the speckled rocks. Salamanders squirmed in the loose peat, and hordes of dragonflies hovered in the air.

Mitsuo turned and asked, "Are your forests like this in America?"

"I've only been to Yosemite. It's pretty nice, except for all the campers," Lincoln said. "Doesn't anyone ever visit this forest?"

Mr. Ono responded, "If they want to pray."

Lincoln thought about this. He liked camping, but walking for five hours wearing a backpack to pray was not what he had expected.

As they rounded a corner, an owl-like bird blinked at Lincoln, then snapped at a dragonfly and caught it.

"Did you see that bird?" Lincoln asked. "He's looking at us."

Mitsuo turned and gazed at the bird. "No, he's looking at you."

And so it seemed to Lincoln. His grandmother always said that birds were a warning, and Lincoln wondered about this bird's message. The bird stared at Lincoln, unblinking.

Lincoln thought of the spider bites. He squeezed his arm hard, but he didn't feel any pain. Still, he wondered whether he had also been bitten and if a stream of poison were flooding his veins and arteries.

"You OK?" Mitsuo asked.

"Yeah. I'm wondering if I got bit, too."

"You would know it," Mitsuo said. "In our country, spider bites are serious. They can kill you." He looked at his father and whispered, "He looks sick, doesn't he?"

Lincoln searched Mr. Ono's face. It was shiny with sweat, but was it sweat from the walk or from poison working in his system? "We'll watch him," Lincoln whispered.

In the quiet of the forest, Lincoln had plenty of time to think of home. He wondered whether it was day or night there. Was his mother at home, watching television with Roy? He wondered what Flaco was doing. Was he in another fight? Was he in trouble for running through the flower bed? Was he missing the late-night handouts Lincoln would give him from the refrigerator? As much as Lincoln had enjoyed his first four weeks in Japan, he was becoming homesick.

———～———

JUST BEFORE NOON, they reached another shrine. A monk was raking leaves with a straw broom. He greeted them in Japanese, and the three of them bowed. Incense made the place smoky and mysterious.

"Cold day," Mr. Ono said, after offering a short prayer at the shrine.

"Yes, cold," the monk said. His teeth were black and his hair was cropped so close that his scalp appeared blue. He wore a white robe and sandals. Prayer beads hung from his wrist.

"This young man is from America," Mr. Ono said, gesturing to Lincoln, who was peeling off his backpack.

"Ah, America!"

"He is studying *kempō* while he's here."

"Ah, *kempō!*" the monk said, smiling. In Japanese, the monk told them he studied with Doshin Do, the founder of *shorinji kempō*. Mitsuo translated for Lincoln.

"You studied with the founder?" Lincoln asked in English. He was impressed.

The monk smiled and blushed faintly.

Mitsuo asked, "Will you please look at my father's arm? He's been bitten."

"Bitten? By an animal?" the monk asked.

"No, a spider," Mitsuo answered.

"It's nothing," Mr. Ono argued.

The monk, putting aside his broom, asked Mr. Ono to take off his shirt. Mr. Ono reluctantly agreed, peeling off his backpack. The monk took the arm into his thin hands and studied the wounds. He pressed the wounds until a squeak of pain escaped Mr. Ono. The bites had grown purplish and hard as tacks.

Mitsuo hovered over the arm. Lincoln stood back, watching the three of them. He knew now that Mr. Ono was seriously hurt.

The monk muttered and scolded Mr. Ono. He said that he should return immediately and seek a doctor. Mr. Ono protested, trying to laugh it off. The priest scolded him again and turned to Mitsuo, warning him that if his father was not cared for he could die.

"Did you hear?" Mitsuo said to his father. "We must go back." He was worried, and so was Lincoln.

"Mitsuo, we should go back," Lincoln agreed. "Right away."

"You are right," Mr. Ono said after a moment. "We should return. I am sorry to ruin our camping trip."

"Forget the camping," Lincoln said. He suddenly felt itchy, as if a spider had nestled under his shirt, puncturing his back with tiny holes. "We better hurry."

They thanked the monk, who bowed and muttered a prayer. He gave them a stick of incense, which was extinguished by a cold wind within a few steps. When they were out of sight of the monk, they crushed it into the ground.

They walked quickly, with the father between the two boys. The walk would take six hours, but luckily it was not yet noon, so they could make it back to the car before nightfall.

"Look at me," the father said, chuckling to himself. "I'm being cared for by children."

"We're not children," Mitsuo said. "Quit joking."

The father offered each of the boys a stick of gum and, mimicking Lincoln, said, "Be cool, *ése.*"

They talked about baseball for a while, then grew silent as they descended the path. They rested twice. By the third rest period, Mr. Ono was covered with sweat. He wanted to take off his jacket, but Mitsuo forced him to keep warm. Mr. Ono shed his backpack, leaving it propped against a rock. Although the boys were hungry, they had to leave the food, nineteen balls of rice in waxed paper.

They walked for three hours. Mr. Ono was now feverish, his armpit swollen as large as a softball. He was tired, and his breathing was shallow.

"Cut it," the father said when they stopped to rest at a small stream. He stripped off his jacket and shirt. "Open it up."

Lincoln and Mitsuo looked at each other. They heard a bird cry in the distance and looked up at the trees. A warning? Lincoln wondered for a moment.

"You mean, cut it open?" Lincoln asked.

"Yes."

"I can't do it."

"I can't do it either," Mitsuo said, looking away. The bird they had heard swooped away with a lizard in its beak.

Lincoln hated the sight of blood. Once he had smashed his thumb in the car door and sprayed blood like a fountain pen. And there had been nosebleeds in playground fights. How many T-shirts had he ruined trying to be brave?

"Cut it!" the father scolded, handing Mitsuo a small knife with a white ivory handle.

Lincoln took the knife and said, "I'll do it." He remembered watching cowboy movies and how one of the snake-bitten cowboys would run a flame over the knife. Lincoln did the same with three matches bunched together. The blue flame licked the nickel-colored blade until it was black with soot. He wiped the soot off with a tissue.

Slowly Lincoln probed the first bite. He tightened his stomach and jaw as the tip of the blade slowly disappeared under the swollen skin. Yellowish blood began to run from the wound, and a small grunt issued from Mr. Ono's mouth. Mr. Ono was gripping a handful of earth, his brow tight from the pain.

"New experience," Mr. Ono said between clenched teeth.

"Don't joke," Mitsuo scolded.

Lincoln turned away, sick. His glance fell on the bird, which was blinking at him.

"Beat it!" Lincoln scolded. The bird flapped its wings and flew away.

Mitsuo took the knife from him and, almost crying, probed the second spider bite. His father watched him as liquid flooded from the wound. Mitsuo squeezed the wound, and more infected blood gushed out.

"Good, son," Mr. Ono said as he started to rise slowly to his feet. "Lincoln-kun, you are a brave boy."

Lincoln, sick with worry, sat on a rock. He didn't feel brave. He felt like he had the time he was jumped by three dudes after a school dance. Scared.

"We should go," Mitsuo said.

Lincoln jumped up when he saw a long-legged spider at his feet. He stomped on the spider and yelled, "Man, they're ugly."

They wrapped the wounds and started off in a hurry. By the time they reached the car, two hours later, it was dusk. Mr. Ono's fever had returned. The boys, now stripped of backpacks, had to drag him between them on their shoulders. They were sweaty and tired, and hunger growled in their stomachs.

They unlocked the car door. Mitsuo looked at Lincoln and asked, "You know how to drive?"

"Me? Drive? I'm fourteen," Lincoln said. He looked at the feverish Mr. Ono. "Yeah. I guess I can figure it out."

They put him in the backseat and wrapped him in a blanket.

Lincoln started the car and, muttering "Here goes," pressed on the gas pedal. The car lurched and slowly advanced from the side of the road onto the empty highway.

Mitsuo found an apple on the seat. He took a bite, and then Lincoln took a bite. "Man, I'm hungry," Lincoln said, his mouth rolling with apple pulp.

"Careful," Mitsuo warned. Lincoln swerved the car, nearly running into a fence. He looked down at the speedometer. He was going thirty-five. That's not too fast, he thought. He remembered going twenty-five on his skateboard, and nearly forty on a ten-speed bike. But he remembered he had crashed both times and skinned up his elbows and knees.

"We must get to that farm town," Mitsuo said, his voice urgent. "There will be a doctor there."

The car bounced when it hit a pothole, and the three of them nearly crashed their heads through the roof.

Mr. Ono muttered something, and Mitsuo lowered his ear to his father. "Quit joking!" Mitsuo exploded. "It's not funny!"

"What did your dad say?" Lincoln asked.

"He says he wants to hear rock music."

"That's what he's going to get," Lincoln said as he flipped on the radio. He worked the steering wheel like the horns of a bull. It was ten miles to that town, and already dark in the unlit mountains where, at night, spiders took over.

13

~~~

LINCOLN WOKE TO see sunlight on the wall, not sure where he was. When he heard the squeak of the oven door in the kitchen, he knew he was back at his second home, the Onos'. He sighed and smacked his lips, refreshed by a hard sleep that had left crust in his eyes. He yawned and opened his eyes wide to find himself face-to-face with a spider large as a black, evil flower. He screamed as he slapped it away, stood up, and whacked it with his jeans.

In the corner of the room, behind a wicker basket of clean clothes, Tony was laughing. "*Carnal*, it's a plastic spider."

Lincoln looked down at the spider. Frowning, he

rolled it over with his toe. Then he picked it up and flung it at Tony.

"I thought I would come see if you were dead or alive," Tony said, coming out from behind the basket.

"That's a dirty trick," Lincoln snapped. "You nearly scared me to death."

"It's a clean joke. A dirty joke would be if I brought you a real spider." Tony picked up Mitsuo's glove, opened it like a mouth, and pounded his fist into it. "I got the lowdown about Mr. Ono."

The lowdown was that Lincoln had driven the car down the narrow road at five thousand feet to a four-lane freeway at one thousand feet. And lived. Mr. Ono still lived, too. He had been unconscious by the time they pulled into Ina and took him to the hospital. There he was laid up in fresh sheets while the boys slept in the car. Mrs. Ono took the train to Ina the next day and brought the boys home, along with her husband, whose arm was in a white sling.

Lincoln put on his jeans and a clean San Francisco Giants T-shirt. He did a few deep knee bends and five push-ups.

"Step back," Tony warned playfully. He bobbed and wove and threw a hook punch. "The *vato* is dangerous."

Mitsuo came into the bedroom and yelled, "Breakfast!" His hands were black and a smear darkened his nose. "How did you sleep, Linc?"

"Like a stone. What's that on your face?"

"Grease, I guess." He swiped at the grease on his nose with the back of his hand. "I took off the fender."

On the way down the mountain, Lincoln had run into a road sign, two fences, and a boulder that had fallen onto the road. He almost ran into a cow. The car was damaged, with one fender buckled beyond repair and the windshield cracked like lightning.

"The fender?"

"Yeah. Dad wants us to take it to the junkyard. He has another one on order."

The three went into the kitchen. Mrs. Ono was cooking eggs and potatoes. "Good morning, hero," she said. "I made something special for you." She peeled back a dish towel to reveal a small stack of steaming tortillas.

"Torts!" Lincoln and Tony shouted.

Mr. Ono came in from the *engawa*. Cigar smoke issued from his mouth in a big white O.

"You smoke cigars?" Lincoln said. He was already slashing a blade of butter across his tortilla.

"I'm celebrating my new life. I hear the spider bite was nothing compared to your crazy driving," he said jokingly.

Mrs. Ono set the plates at the kitchen counter. "I called your mother," she said. "You are lucky to have a nice mother."

"My mother?"

"Yes. I got the recipe for tortillas from your mother. She says everything is nice. And I spoke to your dog, Flaco."

"You spoke to him?"

"Yes. He barked and I barked back."

They laughed and pulled up their chairs. The tortillas disappeared in a hundred chomps.

After breakfast, Tony returned home, leaving Lincoln and Mitsuo to take off the cracked windshield. They raised screwdrivers and began working at the rubber seal, careful not to rip it.

Mr. Ono watched from the porch, basking in the rays of the morning sun. He drank iced tea, sipping its coolness slowly. He barked commands and chewed on his cigar, but not once did he get up to help. He was feeling as lazy as a cat stretched out in sunlight.

After twenty minutes of surgery, the windshield popped off. Mitsuo and Lincoln felt giddy. They wiped their sweaty faces and drank long and hard from the garden hose.

"I have a nice surprise for you when you two come back," Mr. Ono said, an unlit cigarette dangling from his mouth. "So hurry. The surprise starts at three."

Lincoln and Mitsuo tied a rope on the fender and placed the windshield on top of it. They dragged their improvised sleigh of car parts up the street. Children followed them, begging for a ride. Dogs followed as well, and an old woman who came out of her house with her hands over her ears. She shouted that the noise of metal against asphalt was driving her crazy. She threw a small stone at the boys, but they only laughed and hurried away.

At the junkyard at the edge of town, Lincoln and Mitsuo nursed sodas, their shirts sticky with sweat, their arms sore, and their palms raw from the rope.

The owner came out from a shed and, eyeing the windshield and fender, muttered in Japanese that the stuff was junk and a tragedy for the environment.

"Junk? Yeah, but quality junk. It came off my dad's Honda," Mitsuo argued. He knew he wasn't going to get much for the car parts, but it didn't hurt to play them up.

The owner waved Mitsuo off and opened his wallet, which was closed with rubber bands. He gave Mitsuo a handful of yen. Mitsuo was going to argue, but the owner's dog began to sniff their legs, growling and baring his fangs all the way to his pinkish gums.

"Nice doggie," Lincoln said as he stepped backward. "Be cool."

The boys backed out of the junkyard, whistling pleasant tunes.

They returned home and told Mitsuo's father that the junk man was cheap. Even his wallet was held together by rubber bands.

Mr. Ono was in the garden, playing a round of backyard golf. The golf club was rusty, and his single golf ball was chipped and yellow as an old tooth. "I'm on vacation. I can't worry about money," he said, concentrating on his putt and the dent in the earth twenty feet away. He swung the club, and the ball raced like a mouse under a cabbage leaf. He looked at the boys and said, "I need practice. Give me a couple of hours, and you'll see."

Mitsuo chased the ball for his father and returned it by rolling it back. Lincoln stopped the golf ball by trapping it under his shoe.

"You said you had a surprise for us," Mitsuo said.

"Yes, a surprise," Mr. Ono said. He brought out his wallet, which was also held closed together with rubber bands. He chuckled and said, "I am like the junk man."

He handed Lincoln and Mitsuo each a ticket.

"Sumo wrestling, Lincoln-kun. It starts at three o'clock."

"Tough!" Lincoln said, studying the *kanji* on the ticket. "Those dudes are heavy. Thanks."

"Four hundred pounds," Mitsuo said. "And sometimes even five hundred pounds."

Lincoln and Mitsuo arrived at two-thirty at the city auditorium, where spectators, mostly men, crowded for seats. The two overhead air conditioners strained to cool the room.

The spectators grunted and muttered when four sumo wrestlers came out wearing purple loincloths. Their hair was pulled back and knotted into buns. Each wrestler had a towel that looked as small as a washcloth on his huge shoulders.

Lincoln was impressed. He could see that the wrestlers were strong and powerful. Their legs and bellies wiggled with fat, but Lincoln was sure that underneath, muscle twisted like steel cables. And he was sure by the way they walked that these men were warriors.

"The contest is short. Maybe a minute," Mitsuo explained. "The object is to push your opponent out of the ring."

The canvas ring was a circle, unroped, raised, and

set under a tasseled canopy. A referee in a ceremonial kimono stepped into the ring and bowed deeply to the spectators. He was followed by two wrestlers, who stared at each other, their eyes narrowed. They clapped their hands and slapped their thighs and stomachs. They feigned attacks. They stomped their bare feet. They threw a white powdery dust into the air and clapped at the dust.

The spectators grew restless with anticipation. The bout began with the wrestlers bowing to the audience and to each other. They stomped their feet, circled, and feinted. Then they were at each other, chest to sweating chest, knocking against each other so hard that their muscles quivered. And as soon as the bout began, it was over. The bigger of the two wrestlers was knocked out of the ring. He stepped off the platform, wiped his sweaty neck, and, Lincoln guessed, was relieved that he hadn't been crushed. The winning sumo wrestler bowed to the applauding crowd, some of whom were on their feet cheering.

"Man, that was quick," Lincoln said to Mitsuo. "It looks easy."

"But it's not."

Two other sumo wrestlers entered the ring and began pacing from one side of the ring to the other. They, too, clapped their hands and slapped their stomachs. As the anticipation rose, the crowd fanning itself into a sweaty storm of emotion, the referee bowed and introduced the "players." One was from Tokyo and the other from Osaka.

The sumo wrestlers bowed deeply and then

circled each other. The player from Tokyo won in thirty-three seconds, or so Lincoln counted on his watch.

"Man, you can't blink," Lincoln said.

"If you blink, you lose," Mitsuo said.

"They're bad, but I'd hate to be that big. I'd have to shop at the Big and Tall shop."

"Yes, they are large. Too large. They say a sumo wrestler can eat twelve bowls of *rāmen* and still be hungry."

"That's a lot of noodles."

They watched four matches and started home, each with a bottle of soda and a comic book of sumo wrestlers autographed by one of the wrestlers who'd been thrown out of the ring.

At home, before dinner, Lincoln and Mitsuo wrestled sumo-style, with their shirts off. They grunted and sweated and smashed against each other's chests. Red welts blossomed on their arms. Toes were stepped on. Heads knocked.

Mr. Ono, shirt off, watched the boys from the *engawa* and waved away flies. "Cheap entertainment for a poor railroad man," he said, his cigarette glowing in the early dusk.

14

A WEEK PASSED with Lincoln working hard at *kempō*. His test was six days away, just one day before he and Tony would board a jet and return to San Francisco. Oyama-*sensei* said that his skill had grown. He was as lean as a cat, and fast. He could snap a kick, punch, and hold his own when he sparred with the black belts.

But his intense drills were not without pain. A bruise the color of an eggplant showed up on his shoulder. A toenail broke off, and a wiggle of blood splashed the grass as he jumped about on one leg, in pain. The middle finger on his left hand was hurt, and he strained his neck trying to break a choke hold. For two days he walked around like Frankenstein, unable to move his neck, and slept sitting up because it hurt when he lay down.

The days passed. The crops were in, and now Lincoln and Mitsuo were selling them in front of the house. They ate some of the vegetables, but mostly they haggled over the prices with housewives, who were tough customers.

One evening Mr. Ono returned from work and announced, "I have a test for you boys." He sucked long and hard on a soda.

They were lying down in the shade of the porch, exhausted from the heat of the day. The flies were thick as smoke, now that some of the vegetables were spoiling.

Mitsuo looked up and asked, "A test?"

"Yes, a test. To see how fast you are. And if you're good listeners."

The boys sat up, curious. They slapped flies from their toes and listened to Mitsuo's father explain that he had hidden a note in Tokyo and that they were to fetch it for him. He said that they would take a train and that they would have to find the note, read it, and follow its instructions. They had to do this in one day and be home before he returned from work. Their reward would be a visit to the country with the boys driving.

Tokyo was 150 miles away from their own town. The distance wasn't a problem; they would ride a bullet train. The problem was finding their way around Tokyo and through the hordes of workers. The problem was getting back on time.

The boys were excited. They punched each other in the stomach. Mitsuo swung a cupped hand at a fly and swatted the poor creature against the porch. The hurt fly buzzed in a circle, whirling its crushed wings.

"I've never been to Tokyo," Lincoln said. "Except the time you picked me up at the airport."

"I've been there plenty of times but never alone. What if we miss our connections back?" Mitsuo asked, somewhat worried.

Mr. Ono lit a cigarette. He inhaled, let out a stream of smoke from his mouth, and said, eyeing Lincoln, "How do you say the American phrase 'That's too bad'?"

Mr. Ono laughed until he coughed. Lincoln and Mitsuo laughed and jumped up and down, wild at the thought of going to Tokyo by themselves.

"What does this note look like?" Mitsuo asked.

"A note folded into a boat," Mr. Ono replied like a prophet.

"Just a note? A paper boat?" Lincoln asked.

"That's it. Just a piece of paper. In a fern. In the Sumitomo Building in the Shinjuku district." Mr. Ono crushed his cigarette and started to leave; when Mitsuo asked him about the building, he waved them off. "Enough clues. We'll see how smart you two are."

Mitsuo knew the Sumitomo Building, a high rise with fifty-two floors. He knew the Shinjuku district. It was where there were small bars and restaurants, a hangout for young students and office workers.

"This is going to be fun," Lincoln said.

"I guess so," Mitsuo muttered, lost in thought.

The fly that he'd swatted was now washing its face, apparently OK. "A paper boat in a fern. My dad's a character."

The next morning they woke before daybreak. They dressed quickly and ate a handful of rice balls on the run.

At 6:45 they arrived at the train station, where Mr. Ono worked as a mechanic. The bullet train was due to leave at 7:10; it was a late train that would stop only twice, to pick up commuters.

"Where are our tickets?" Mitsuo asked.

"You get no tickets. You boys get to ride with the mail and chickens."

"You mean in the back?" Mitsuo asked.

"I like it," Lincoln said, beaming. He had been on trains three times, but never in the mail compartment.

"But we won't be able to look out."

"Good, then you can close your eyes and go to sleep."

Mr. Ono scooted the boys to the cargo car. He slid open the door to a mountain of bagged mail and stacks of newspapers.

"Welcome to your new home." He chuckled. He gave the boys three thousand yen and handed them return tickets, warning them if they lost these then they would have to stay in Tokyo for good. They would have to work as dishwashers to get the money to come back.

Mitsuo hopped into the train and Lincoln followed. Mr. Ono gave the boys a stiff salute and closed

107

the door. Within minutes the train started, slowly at first, but then picking up speed until it jerked along at 110 miles per hour.

A small overhead light went on after the door was closed. The boys got comfortable and sat on the bags, then opened one of them. They pulled out comic books. Lincoln liked the pictures of Japanese super-heroes, all with cuts of muscle that would put Olympic athletes to shame.

For a second they thought of opening a package. They knew it was food, but they also knew it was a crime to open someone else's mail and they were scared of being arrested. So they only sniffed the package, Lincoln guessing that it held plums and Mitsuo guessing dried fish.

There was a small, greasy window high in a corner. Lincoln stacked a couple of mailbags against the wall and climbed up to the window. He stared out at farmland broken up with smoke. In the distance, he could see a mountain dotted with remnants of snow. And snow was what Lincoln was thinking about. The cargo car was heating up. The air grew thick and wet. The boys were sweating and dry-mouthed. Lincoln pulled a stick of gum out of his pocket and tore it in half to share.

"What do you think your father is hiding?" Lincoln asked, unbuttoning the front of his shirt.

"Probably money. He likes to give money away."

"I wish my mom was generous with money." Lincoln recalled being caught going through her coin purse. He recalled the race around the living room and her yelling, "You little thief!" Little did she know that he had been pinching $1.20 for a Mother's Day gift.

When the train pulled into Tokyo, they opened the cargo door and peeked out, scared that someone might scold them for going "baggage." There were enough witnesses: thousands of commuters hurrying to work.

"We could jump and run," Lincoln suggested.

"Why not?" Mitsuo agreed.

Counting, "*Ichi, ni, san, shi, go,*" they dropped to the platform, arms out like wings. A security guard turned when he heard their grunting fall. He shouted at them to stay, but the boys took off. The guard ran after them, weaving in and out of the crowd, but Lincoln and Mitsuo were too lean, too quick, too full of fear to let themselves get caught. They ran a half mile, stopped, and sat on a curb where a pigeon with a crooked beak was drinking from a small oily puddle.

"Let's get a Coke," Mitsuo suggested, breathing hard. It was nine-thirty, and already the asphalt was wavering with the summer heat.

"Good idea," Lincoln said.

They bought sodas at a newsstand and drank slowly while looking at comic books. Finished, Mitsuo asked the cashier about the Sumitomo Building. The cashier waved his hand, muttered in guttural Japanese, and shook his head at the boys for reading his comic books without buying one.

"Oh no." Mitsuo groaned. "We got off at the wrong stop. It's on the other side of the city!"

"The other side! What should we do?"

"Take a bus," Mitsuo suggested. "Let's go."

They boarded a bus, but it was going in the wrong direction, and they ended up traveling six blocks farther away from the Sumitomo Building. The ride cost them twenty minutes and two tokens.

"How come you didn't tell us?" Mitsuo yelled at the driver in Japanese.

The bus driver yelled at Mitsuo, telling him to get off the bus. Mitsuo answered back, and the bus driver picked up the telephone to call his station.

"What a slimeball," Lincoln muttered under his breath. He wanted to drop the driver, but he knew better.

The boys started to get off the bus, but the driver cut the engine. The door wouldn't open. The air-conditioning groaned to a stop. All exits were blocked. The driver got out of his seat with an ugly sneer.

Lincoln spotted two policemen trying to cross against the traffic to their side of the street. They were wearing white gloves and looked very clean in spite of the heat—and very determined.

"Push, Mitsuo! *¡La policía!*" Lincoln yelled. Lincoln and Mitsuo heave-hoed, and the door sighed open just as the bus driver grabbed Mitsuo's sleeve.

Without thinking, Lincoln used a *kempō* technique to free Mitsuo, hitting a pressure point in the bus driver's forearm. The bus driver screamed in pain and dropped to his knees.

"Now I did it," Lincoln said. "*¡Ándale,* Mitsuo!"

They darted from the bus, kicking their legs high and pumping their arms. When they looked back, the two cops were only a block behind. Lincoln and Mitsuo turned on the juice, their lungs sucking in Tokyo's heat.

The boys ducked into the subway and leaped onto a train that carried them, along with their worry, near the Sumitomo Building.

Once they left the subway and were at street level, the heat blasted them like a furnace. The sharp sunlight hurt their eyes. Mitsuo asked for directions from a woman selling flowers under a striped awning. The roses seemed to gasp for air, and the daisies were hanging their heads, exhausted. She pointed to a nearby building, an unusual triangular building tall enough to block out the sun.

On their way the boys were ever watchful for police in blue uniforms. They seemed to be every-where. Directing traffic at clogged intersections, standing before storefronts, peeking into alleys, and scolding kids crossing the street against red lights. When Lincoln and Mitsuo stopped to buy another soda, they turned to look directly into a policeman's eyes, and he seemed to know that Lincoln was a crim-inal, an American kid with brown skin who had pushed open a door to avoid an irate bus driver and then dropped him with a painful strike at a pressure point.

A lump of fear and some soda washed down Lin-coln's throat when the policeman turned and walked away.

111

"Here we are," Mitsuo said.

They started to enter the lobby, but quickly backed out when a security guard looked at them hard. The building was all business, not a place for kids in sneakers, and especially not for teenagers who were going to rake their hands through a planter looking for a piece of paper folded into a boat.

"This is going to be difficult," Mitsuo said, looking back into the lobby. He spied four planters near the elevators.

"Yeah. How do we get in there?"

"I got it," Mitsuo said. "We just look like we belong to one of the people going in."

They turned and watched people entering the revolving doors: businessmen in heat-crumpled suits, office workers, and delivery people.

"There," Mitsuo said, pointing to an older woman. "We follow her in."

Mitsuo and Lincoln skipped into step behind the woman. Once they were in the lobby, Mitsuo struck up a conversation in rapid Japanese with her. He babbled on and on so that the security guard would not become suspicious. But he talked so much, so loudly, that the security guard looked over at them.

Mitsuo asked the woman about the fern in the nearest planter. She walked over to the fern and looked at it, puzzled, then looked at the boys. While she responded to Mitsuo's question, Mitsuo and Lincoln casually raked their hands over the soil: nothing. Mitsuo asked her about another fern, but she just gave him an odd look and started walking toward the elevator. Lincoln glanced at the security guard, who was tying his shoe and studying the three of them.

Mitsuo and Lincoln gave up on creating a distraction and rushed to the next fern. They plowed the earth with their fingers, coming up with leaves, rocks, and small pebbles, but no white paper boat. Mitsuo looked up to see the security guard walking toward them.

"Let's check the planter over there," Mitsuo said. They rushed over, raked the dirt, and searched among the leaves.

The guard was now hovering above them. Just as he started to question them, Lincoln parted a fan of leaves and screamed, "I got it!" He was staring at a piece of soggy paper shaped more like a hat than a boat.

He snatched it as they backed away from the guard, then darted for the exit, Lincoln first with Mitsuo at his heels.

The heat struck them as they raced away, the guard behind them, blowing his whistle and shouting for them to stop. Two cops eating *rāmen* at a stand-up eatery at the corner looked but didn't join the chase.

The boys ran three blocks, then stopped in an alley to catch their breath. Their shirts were soaked. The guard had been left far behind.

Mitsuo unfolded the piece of paper to find only an amateurish drawing of a clown. He turned it over, at first baffled, then as mad as a cat dunked in water. There was nothing on the paper, except the clown with three large teeth.

"What kind of joke is this?" Lincoln asked.

Mitsuo tossed away the piece of paper, which appeared to laugh at them as it fell to the ground. "My father is a joker."

As they started down the street, they were spotted by the two policemen who had been eating *rāmen* outside the Sumitomo Building. One pointed and shouted at them.

"Like hell," Lincoln said, fists doubled.

"Like hell," Mitsuo mimicked. "In your face!"

They outran the policemen and made their way to the subway that would take them to the train station. It was quarter to three. The train ride would take an hour and a half, which would bring them back to Atami two hours before Mitsuo's father would get home from work. They would be glad to get out of Tokyo. The place was too dangerous, and they were exhausted.

They boarded the train, this time in the passenger section, and fell asleep ten minutes after it pulled out of the station.

———◇———

AT HOME, MR. Ono was already on the *engawa*, nursing an iced tea. He had come home from work two hours early so that he would be sure to beat the boys. "You two clowns look tired," he said as he rested his iced tea on his stomach.

"That was a terrible joke!" Mitsuo yelled as he closed the gate behind him. "A clown face."

"A clown face? What are you talking about?" Mr. Ono asked innocently. He fanned himself with a newspaper, holding back laughter.

"You know!" they both yelled. They threw themselves down on the steps. Their necks were sunburned and their heads hurt from too much sun.

"There must be a mistake. You did not find my little note?" A wave of laughter broke from his throat. The iced tea jiggled and spilled on his stomach.

They ate dinner, and when the evening cooled, Mitsuo's father suggested that they go for a ride. Three miles outside of town, he pulled over and said, "You first, Mitsuo. Drive me around."

The boys were excited. Mitsuo started the car, revving the engine so that blue smoke stank up the air. He put the car into gear, and outside of town, out of view of his mother—and Lincoln's mother, and the police—they drove over the country road, utterly happy that they were fourteen.

15

AFTER A TWO-HOUR practice, after a hundred kicks and punches, after the armlocks that sent pain shooting up to the elbows, after the rolls over the grass of the outdoor dojo, Oyama-*sensei* took Lincoln aside. She plucked at his hair and said, "It is too long again. Cut before you promote."

Lincoln touched his hair. It had grown in the six weeks he had been in Japan. The first week, Mrs. Ono had cut it so close that his scalp showed. Now, in the middle of August, it was getting shaggy as a mop and nearly as stinky after a fierce workout.

Lincoln's promotion to *nikkyu* would be tomorrow evening. He was nervous. He knew the techniques, but he was still scared that he might disappoint his teacher. He was scared that he might do his *embu*, his prearranged form, terribly wrong. And he was scared that he might lose his match. This promotion meant he would have to spar, and there was no telling if he would leave Japan with his teeth in his pocket.

"Do you think I'm ready?" Lincoln asked.

"Don't talk like that. Be confident." Oyama-*sensei* walked away, untying her black belt. "Cut your hair by tomorrow." She disappeared into the house, leaving him in the yard, where he practiced his *embu* some more before dressing.

When he got home, Mitsuo was watching television. Bart Simpson was speaking Japanese. His duck lips seemed to sync up perfectly in his goofy tirade against his father.

"Where's your mom and dad?" Lincoln asked.

"They're at the movies," Mitsuo said, turning off the television. "Let's go for a walk."

Lincoln was tired, but he couldn't say no. He was going to miss Mitsuo, and he was going to miss Japan.

He felt better after a quick shower. Mitsuo was waiting for him on the *engawa*, and they left the yard and walked up the street. Atami, their farm town, smelled of harvest: cucumbers, radishes, cabbage, tomatoes, and acres of rice sacked and ready for shipment.

"*Sushi o tabemashō*," Lincoln read from his secondhand book of Japanese as they walked. He wanted to learn as much Japanese as he could before he left. "Yeah, I wouldn't mind eating *sushi*." He looked down at the next sentence and whispered,

"*Nani ō sashiagemasu ka?* What should I give you?" Lincoln muttered his lessons, and now and then Mitsuo corrected him.

They passed the *sentō*. They could hear the spill of water from the faucets and men talking loudly about the day's work. They passed the bars, where men sipped sake and filled the air with cigarette smoke. They passed the *pachinko* palace, where the pinball-like game thundered with steel balls. They tried to sneak inside to play a game, but they were chased out by a man with tattoos running up and down his arms like snakes.

They crossed the street and walked up an alley. Near a Zen temple, they saw a man trying to pry open the door of a bicycle shop. The man thought he was hidden by shadow, but he glowed fluorescent blue from the light of a nearby drugstore.

Lincoln and Mitsuo quietly watched as the man pried at the door, which was locked in three places. After each noisy try, the man paused, looked around, and then returned his attention to prying open the locks. He gave up when someone walked past, a man click-clacking in his *geta*. The would-be thief left, and Lincoln and Mitsuo followed him. They moved from car to car, car to tree, tree to building.

"This is cool," Lincoln said under his breath. "I feel like a detective."

"Like on 'Miami Vice,'" Mitsuo agreed.

The man entered a bar where the entrance was covered with a bead curtain. Lincoln whispered, "Let's see what he's doing."

They crossed the street, looked in through the small window, and saw the bartender pouring sake into a white bowl.

Lincoln and Mitsuo jumped when they heard their names. They turned around and saw Mitsuo's parents, who were just returning home from the movie.

"What are you two doing?" Mrs. Ono asked. "Why are you looking in the bar?"

The boys' faces blazed with embarrassment. Neither could say anything for a moment.

"We were just looking," Lincoln finally said feebly.

"If you are so interested, we should go in," Mr. Ono said.

"But it's a bar," Mitsuo said. "We're not allowed."

"Then why are you looking in?" his mother scolded.

"I know the owner. He gets free train rides from me," Mr. Ono said. He entered, and the others followed, the beaded curtain clicking as they parted it.

The bar was smoky. Crates of beer and sake stood in the corner. An aquarium with gurgling green water but no fish stood near the cash register.

Mr. Ono greeted the owner with a smile, a short bow, and an explanation that Lincoln was from California and it was almost his last night in Japan. They were there to celebrate.

The owner bowed and showed them to a low table, where they were served drinks: sodas for the boys, tea for Mrs. Ono, and sake for Mr. Ono.

Lincoln and Mitsuo looked around. Two men sat in the corner playing *go*. Others sat alone, nursing their drinks.

"Which one do you think he is?" Mitsuo asked in Lincoln's ear. Lincoln shrugged his shoulders and said, "Beats me." They felt giddy knowing they were sitting near a thief, or at least a potential thief.

They left the bar without paying, the owner insisting because it was the end of Lincoln's stay in Japan. Mr. Ono bowed, this time deeply, and Lincoln bowed as well and said, *"Arigatō gozaimasu."* He looked back at the two men sitting at the bar. Neither one smiled or bowed. One of them crushed his cigarette and immediately lit up another. Lincoln concluded that they were both thugs.

———

THE NEXT DAY, Lincoln woke up early. He practiced *kempō* in the yard, the kicks and punches, the armlocks and throws, and his *embu*.

Mrs. Ono washed Lincoln's clothes and packed them in his suitcase. The following morning, Saturday, he and Tony would be on a plane to San Francisco.

After lunch he let Mitsuo cut his hair. Mitsuo snipped and tugged and made Lincoln scream, "You're killing me!"

Mr. Ono took over, and when he finished and whisked the snips of hair from Lincoln's shoulders, Lincoln's head was nearly as bald as a fist.

Lincoln and Mitsuo sat on the *engawa*, quiet.

They knew they were about to leave each other, these brothers from different countries. A mosquito landed on Lincoln's arm, but instead of swatting it away, he let it drink. Tomorrow, when he was on the plane, he would look down at his arm and remember that mosquito and remember sitting with Mitsuo on the *engawa*.

"You'll have to come and visit us," Lincoln said.

Mitsuo agreed that the next time they would meet in California. He wanted to go to America's Disneyland, which he thought must be even better than Tokyo's Disneyland. Lincoln said that Disneyland was fine, but what he wanted to do with Mitsuo was go surfing in Santa Cruz. He had always wanted to try surfing, but his mother wouldn't let him. If Mitsuo were with him, maybe she would break down and drive them to Santa Cruz.

"Yeah, you could cross the Pacific and see Tony and me," Lincoln said. He described the Mission District, Chinatown, Italian food, American cars, the Bay Bridge, the Golden Gate Bridge, the 49ers, and the Giants—all the life that breathed around the San Francisco Bay.

After dinner, Lincoln excused himself and said that he was going to *kempō* practice. Mr. and Mrs. Ono wanted to go, knowing that tonight he would test. But Lincoln was nervous and said that he didn't want them to see how terrible he was.

"You are a strong boy," Mrs. Ono said. She had washed and ironed his *gi*. It looked sharp as it lay on his bed.

"You will be bad." Mitsuo punched Lincoln in the arm, and Lincoln punched him back.

"Nah, I'm going to stink up the place, really."

Mr. Ono told him that he would do well. In the end, however, Lincoln persisted and they let him go alone.

They waved to Lincoln from the gate as he walked up the street. Sadness gathered in his throat. He wanted to run back and beg them, "Please, come and watch." But he couldn't. He kicked a rock, and it went flying.

At practice, Lincoln warmed up while Oyama-*sensei* stood watching. She called her students together. Three of them were being promoted: Lincoln and two boys about his age. The first part, the basic kicks and punches, went well. He could hear his sleeve snap beautifully. He could feel his punch extend and recoil, his kick extend and recoil. He pictured himself: a brown boy in a white *gi*, five thousand miles from home.

Lincoln struggled some with the pins and arm-locks, and had to repeat his *embu*. The first time, he had fallen face first into the grass. When he got up, bits of grass clung to his tongue. He swallowed and continued, less than perfect but good enough to make two black belts nod their heads approvingly.

Oyama-*sensei* asked them to put on their gloves. The picture of himself once again appeared in his mind's eye. He felt strong. Sweat blotted the back of his uniform. He saluted his opponent, a boy with shaved hair, and approached him carefully. Now is the

122

time, Lincoln told himself. This is what you've practiced for.

Lincoln circled, and his first blow landed against his opponent's shoulder. Lincoln took a blow to his ear, and then they were on top of each other, kicking and punching. They broke and circled slowly. *Kempō* was lifelong. Lincoln knew this, and his opponent, who was bleeding from the nose, knew this. Why hurry?

16

LINCOLN PEERED OUT of the small window that was flecked with drops of rain. The Pacific Ocean was thirty-five thousand feet down, flashing like a knife in the late-evening sun. He and Tony were seven hours into their return trip home. They had eaten twice and watched one movie, a comedy neither thought was funny.

Lincoln reclined his seat and looked at Tony, who was asleep with his mouth open and headphones on his ears. When Lincoln pulled off the headphones, Tony didn't even stir. He snored softly.

Lincoln recalled the sparring match with the boy his age, a boy whose hair, like Lincoln's, was cut so short that his scalp showed, a forest of bristles. Lincoln had passed to *nikkyu* rank, two steps from black belt. But he had been slammed around: his left eye was bruised, his lip was swollen, and a kick in the arm and one in the ribs had left him hurting. He had gotten his breath knocked out of him with a front snap kick. But on the lawn that was their dojo, in the presence of six black belts kneeling around the ring, and on his next-to-last day in Japan, Lincoln hadn't been able to double over and crumple to the grass. He was full of pride, Mexican pride. He wasn't going to be a push-over. So he took that kick, and the other blows. He took them and gave some back. The kid got a nose-bleed and almost went down when Lincoln got him with a side kick. Only after the match did he find out the boy's name: Yoshi.

Lincoln had bowed deeply, and Yoshi had bowed back. "You will be very good one day," Yoshi said, breathing hard.

"You, too," Lincoln panted.

That was yesterday. Now he and Tony were returning home with gifts for their parents, and gifts for themselves. Lincoln's Japanese parents had given him a pair of *geta*, and Mitsuo had given him two bottles of *ramune*, which he had promised to save until Mitsuo visited San Francisco. They would toast themselves and toast their families—and then hit the streets of the Mission District.

Lincoln had been weak with sadness in the morning when he saw Mrs. Ono snap his suitcase closed, his suitcase that was bloated with clothes, gifts, and a new *kempō gi*, a gift from Oyama-*sensei*. He fought back tears as the Onos drove him and Tony to the airport, as the farmland gave way to houses and factories. At the airport he gave the Onos *abrazos*, deep hugs of love, and promised them real Mexican food when they stepped onto the shores of California.

"Come back soon," Mrs. Ono cried. She eyed Lincoln's hair and combed it with her fingers. "Your hair grows like a bush, Lincoln-kun. What will your mother say if we send you back with hair to your feet?"

Lincoln smiled.

"Yes, come back and I will let you drive my car," Mr. Ono joked. "It will be a big American car—Cadillac."

Lincoln and Tony shook hands with Mitsuo *raza*-style, heaved their carry-on bags onto their shoulders, and departed through Gate 93.

Six weeks since he'd been home. Lincoln was thinking about his mother, a hard worker who kept him clothed and fed, and about his dog, Flaco. His Japanese parents were special, too, Mrs. Ono with her tenderness, Mr. Ono with his rough kindness and off-beat jokes. And now a brother, Mitsuo.

Lincoln looked out the window again. The sun had almost disappeared and far, far below was the Pacific Ocean. What life could be better than the one he was living?

SPANISH WORDS AND PHRASES

abrazo—hug

adios—good-bye

amigo—friend

¡andale!—hurry up!

¡ay, caramba!—an exclamation similar to "oh, wow!"

barrio—neighborhood

¡callate!—be quiet!

carnal—blood brother, good friend

chango—pest

chavalo—boy

Chicano—person of Mexican descent

cholos—gang members

¿entiendes?—do you understand?

es muy rico—it's delicious

ése—dude, guy

está bien—it's OK

familias—families

frijoles—mashed beans

gente—people

hace mucho calor—it's very hot

la migra—immigration authorities

La Noche de Guadalajara—The Guadalajara Night

la policía—police or policeman

Mechista—a member of the college political group MEChA (*Movimiento Estudiantil Chicano de Aztlán*)

mi'jo—my son (affectionate)

mis—my (pl.)

moco—mucus

mole—chili sauce for meat

nalgas—buttocks

no, chavalo, su amigo es lindo y listo—no, boy, your friend is handsome and smart

¡órale!—all right!

¡órale, ése!—all right, dude!

¡órale, Papi!—all right, Dad!

pues sí—well, yes

raza—Latino people

sandalias—sandals

señorita, mi amigo es muy feo y un tonto también—lady, my friend is very ugly and a fool, also

simón que sí, Papi—of course, Dad

tía—aunt

tío—uncle

vato—dude

vato loco—crazy dude

veteranos—war veterans

vieja—old woman

¡Viva la Raza!—Hurray for the Mexican people!

JAPANESE WORDS AND PHRASES

anata no tan 'joobi wa itsu desu ka?—when is your birthday?

arigatō gozaimasu—thank you very much

chichi—the speaker's father

dojo—training ground or school for martial arts

dōzo—please

embu—planned attacks, drill

engawa—porch

futon—Japanese fold-up bed

gaijin—non-Japanese person

gasshō—salute

geta—wooden slippers

gi—martial-arts uniform

go—board game similar to checkers

go—five

hachimaki—cloth headband

haha—the speaker's mother

hai—yes

hashi—chopsticks

ichi—one

ima Atami ni sun'de imasu—I am now living in Atami

Jizō—the saint who protects children

juhō—grabbing and pinning techniques

kanji—Japanese characters used in writing

karakoro—clickety-clackety

katana—sword

kempō—a martial art

-kun—ending to a personal name used between peers or by a superior, e.g. a parent to a child

kyu—level

mimikaki—ear pick

nasu—eggplant

ni—two

nigirimeshi—rice balls

nikkyu—second rank

ohayō—good morning

pachinko—a pinball-like game

rāmen—noodles

ramune—a popular soft drink

sake—rice wine

samurai—a noble warrior

san—three

sankyu—brown-belt rank

sensei—teacher

sentō—public bath

shi—four

shorinji kempō—a martial art

sumo—a type of wrestling in which the object is to push or throw the opponent out of the ring

sushi o tabemashō—let's eat sushi

tatami—straw mats

yen—Japanese money

yukata—cotton kimono